# Just Another *African* Adventure

## By

## Jane Maxwell

RedSox Press, Solihull

Available from Amazon.com and other retail outlets

Available on Kindle and other devices

# 'Just Another African Adventure'

Published by RedSox Press 2016

www.redsoxpress.co.uk

ISBN 978-0-9935355-0-5

RedSox Press Limited Reg. No. 09863441

Type: Garamond

Printed by CreateSpace

# Just Another African Adventure

# Prologue

*THE SHRILL CONTINUOUS blast of a siren split the air as a fire engine turned in through the hospital gates pulling up close to the building. A ladder was hastily extended to reach the second floor parapet where a figure desperately clung to a buttress with a foot on either side. Ellen looked on, her heart in her mouth, as a fire man shinned up the ladder. She'd been called out of a swimming lesson by the school secretary and told to get to the General Hospital where there was an emergency. She hadn't known what it was, but she knew it had to concern Daniel. Who else would it be? She held her breath, her face pale, whilst the fireman quietly spoke words of encouragement to her husband who was wearing a white hospital gown which flapped around his legs. He was plainly terrified. After what seemed like an eternity the fireman managed to persuade him to move one foot, then the other, onto the ladder and very slowly he guided Daniel down to the ground where a male nurse was waiting to rush him into the building in a wheelchair.*

*Ellen followed them inside and heard the Ward Sister giving instructions to take the patient to Ward 12. She ran over and put her arms around Daniel. His shoulders were shaking as he wept.*

*'I'm so sorry Ell. I'm so sorry,' tears streaming down his once handsome face which was now gaunt and grey.*

*'Sh. It's alright, Lovie. I'm here' she soothed.' He was like a frightened child in the dark holding on to her hand so tightly she thought he'd never let go. Everything he'd done was forgiven as she looked at that pitiful figure of the man she loved and who had once been so proud.*

*She walked beside the wheelchair down the long bleak corridors and thought back to their early days in Lusaka when Daniel had been so handsome and sure of himself. Life had been carefree and full of hope then. But Life could also be cruel. Everything had been perfect once upon a time. How could things have become this desperate in five years?*

*Pictures of the past flooded her mind; of sitting in the car in the rain swept lane outside her parents' house; Eric telling her quite suddenly, two weeks before their wedding day, when all the invitations had been sent out, that he'd made a mistake and wasn't ready to tie himself down. Then the blue airmail letter arriving from her old school chum, Sally, suggesting she might like to spend some time in Zambia. 'A new beginning' she'd called it. At the time there had been headline news about the troubles in that part of the world and she wasn't sure if she should go. The media made it sound really dangerous. Blood would be running down the streets according to the Daily Express. But having* sat at the kitchen table mulling it over with her philosophical mother she'd decided that she could always get back on the plane and come home if things looked really bad, so she'd packed in her teaching job at the primary school, sold her V.W. and left home on a bleak wintery morning in December, making her way to Heathrow on the train from Central Station to start a new life; a life that did not include Eric.

Ellen continued walking next to the wheelchair holding Daniel's hand. He'd calmed down somewhat and now sat hunched up looking very woebegone. The nurse stopped at a door and pressed a bell. A male orderly came to unlock it and held it open as Daniel was wheeled through into a large social area where patients were involved in various pursuits. Some were playing board games, others reading books, most just sat around vacantly smoking and drinking tea. They'd arrived at Ward 12, the psychiatric ward. The nurse wheeled the chair through to a long bedded room where he helped his patient into a newly made bed. Daniel reached out and Ellen felt his hand trembling in hers. Could this be the same confident man who'd set her heart a-flutter years before? She recalled the day she arrived in Lusaka and wondered where it had all gone so badly wrong.

# Chapter 1

December 1967

THE 6000 MILE journey in the propeller driven aeroplane was long and tedious stopping twice to refuel at Entebbe and Benghazi, but after twenty-two hours the plane eventually touched down in Lusaka. Ellen remembered the feeling of excitement, as a wall of humidity hit her at the door of the aircraft. Canvas bag in hand, she stepped down into an unfamiliar, yet exhilarating new world.

The African sun blazed like molten gold in a brilliant blue sky as she walked the short distance across the heat hazed tarmac and entered the airport building, a strange looking low structure with a rounded roof, more like an army Nissan hut than an airport. She was like a child observing every detail; the black porters lethargically unloading luggage from a trailer; the Immigration Official lazily checking her passport with a careless gesture of dismissal; Customs Officers chatting in a strange tongue and rumbling with laughter at some private joke. No haste, just an overall sense of carefree abandon.  It all seemed so far away from the hustle and bustle of her native Manchester and the heartache of a broken romance.

Expats, eager for diversion and the latest news from home, pressed forward at the barrier, awaiting friends and relatives visiting from Overseas.  Then she recognized Ben in faded khaki shorts and aertex t-shirt.  She hadn't seen him since his wedding to Sally five years before but he was as big as she remembered him.  He spotted her and waved, then bounded easily over the barrier.

'Hey Ellen,' he boomed in his deep cultured voice, 'I hardly recognised you.  You've changed your hairstyle.'  He wrapped her in a generous hug.

'Sally and the kids are waiting back at the farm.  The kids are hopping up and down like demented rabbits and Sally has checked your room at least half a dozen times.'

She laughed at his droll description of his young family.

'I can't believe I'm here, Ben.  *You* haven't changed a bit. I'd recognize that voice anywhere.'

'You must be tired.  Come on.  Let's get you back to the house.'

He led her to a battle scarred Rover motor car parked askew outside the main entrance, loaded her brand new shiny suitcase into the boot and slammed it shut.  Ellen breathed in the mellow aroma of old leather as she lowered herself into the passenger seat.

They set off down dusty avenues lined with low slung homes on sprawling plots, their breeze block patio walls dripping with orange honeysuckle and deep red bougainvillea. A balmy breeze wafting through the open car windows was filled with the heady fragrances of frangipani and magnolia, jasmine and mimosa.

Soon they were driving down the wide main street of Lusaka, with its central reservation of squat flamboyant trees topped with fiery blossoms. African women wearing colourful turbans, sat cross-legged in the shade, suckling their round bellied infants. Shops lining the street were busy with housewives wearing pretty cotton dresses, and a pavement market was alive with vendors selling everything from bananas to Bombay silks. A wizened old madala crouched on the footpath haggling over the price of his carved kudu, decorative drums and tribal masks, whilst two plump matrons sat gossiping and crocheting nearby, entreating wandering tourists to buy their lace tablecloths and beaded necklets.

At the end of the main street they turned right at a large traffic island adorned with cheerful red cannas and stately blue agapanthus and soon they were accelerating along twin ribbons of tarmacked strip road, which continued for miles out into open countryside and the hazy blue hills beyond. The road was now bordered by corrugated tin shacks with an occasional circular, thatched mud dwelling breaking the monotony. Brown hens foraged for seed in the dust, and the long, ragged leaves of corn cob plants fluttered in a gentle breeze.

Shortly they left the town behind, and there were acres of farmland on either side of them. An abandoned red tractor was left to rust at the edge of a field, whilst an expanse of unregimented maize plants waited to be harvested in another.

After several miles, they reached the end of the tarmac and bumped onto a sand road. The heavy motorcar churned up clouds of red dust and Ellen's nostrils were filled with the warm, earthy odour of the bush. Ben told her they were not far away from his smallholding.

A mile or so further on they turned off down a rugged cart track. The car rattled and bumped mercilessly over ruts and stones for half a mile alongside uncultivated bush-land, until, at last, it pulled up next to a green roofed bungalow, fronted by full length windows and a wide raised terrace. A rounded kopje, covered in straggly trees, stood guard nearby.

Everything was still in the lunchtime heat except for the shrill intermittent chirruping of a solitary cricket...

Suddenly dogs were barking and children shrieking. There was a clamour of excitement as two English bull terriers and four blond bare footed urchins wearing shorts and nothing else, came bursting around the side of the house to greet them shrieking with childish glee. Her friend Sally came hurrying out, a cotton shift covering her ample frame, her round face beaming with delight. She hugged Ellen tight, 'It's so good to have you here at last, Ellen. Can't wait to hear all your news'. It had been six years since they'd seen each other. They'd been at school together, got into teenage scrapes, and spent time at one another's houses and slept top and tail in a single bed sharing their problems about boyfriends until well after midnight. Before Sally's wedding they had told one another everything and Ellen had missed her friend, especially after the break up with Eric. Sally had gone out with Eric briefly whilst they were all still at school, but then at seventeen she'd met Ben at a Young Farmers' dance, who was right for her in every way. She was bossy and liked everything done her way whist Ben was big and cumbersome, slow to anger and dependable. But if Sally pushed him too far he'd erupt like a volcano and she knew the signs so didn't push his boundaries. It was a shock to Ellen to hear they were off to Zambia soon after their marriage but Sal told her the money was good and at the time they had no children. But soon after arriving in Zambia

Sal had become pregnant with Darren and over the past five years they'd produced three more in quick succession, Gemma and twins Will and Sarah. Ben adored Sally and was proud of his brood. He was her sturdy rock whilst Sally was his motivator. Together they were a team.

The children were jumping up and down around her with excitement. A foreign aunty visiting was as good as E.T. Ellen was over whelmed. Once she had lifted and hugged each lively little body in turn she laughingly told them, 'Tomorrow morning when I've unpacked there's a little present for each of you.' The children could hardly contain themselves. Once the hub bub had died down Sally took control.

'Calm down now. Let Aunty Ellen relax for a bit,' she said briskly. 'Ben, are we having a braai? I've got boerewors and steak in the fridge.'

'No problem. Come on kids,' boomed Ben, rallying his troops, 'Let's go climb the kopje and collect some firewood.'

They disappeared around the back of the farmhouse and Sally hugged her friend again. 'I can't believe you're here at last. We're going to have such fun. Ben will be away on business a lot advising farmers out in the bush. He can be out two or three nights a week sometimes and it'll be good to have some adult company for a change. I want to hear all

about the break up with Eric. I have to say I was always a
bit doubtful when you wrote and said you were getting
married. He was a good-looking bloke but shallow. You're
better off without him, Love.'

She linked arms with her friend and led her inside talking
excitedly about what they would do the following day.

'First we shall talk and talk and talk. Then we need to go
into town and see if we can get you a job in one of the local
schools. Then we'll go and have lunch at the Kawena Hills
Hotel. They do good chicken in the basket there. And
afterwards we'll come home and have a swim and I'll get
Enoch to cook us something nice for supper.'

'Stop!' cried Ellen laughing. 'Let me take it all in.
Who's Enoch?'

'He's my domestic rock but don't tell Ben that,' she
grinned cheekily, 'Enoch and his wife Esta live in the kia
behind the house.' Sally pointed vaguely towards the back
of the house. She had difficulty talking without waving her
hands constantly to emphasise her meaning. 'That's a little
house by the way. Don't know what I'd do without them.
Enoch's food is the best you've ever tasted. What he can't
do with a pound of mince isn't worth knowing about. And
Esta is wonderful with the kids. They love her to bits.
They've been away in their village for the past two weeks and

we've really missed them.'  She paused for breath whilst Ellen took in her surroundings.

Inside it was pleasantly cool.  Ellen was intrigued by the huge gas fridge in the roomy farmhouse kitchen.  Sally explained that out there in the bush without mains services they needed a generator for the lights, gas bottles for fridge and cooker and their own borehole for water.  They had to be self-sufficient but sometimes it could be inconvenient if the generator ran out of petrol or the gas bottles failed to arrive on time.  Then they would have to cook on the braai outside until Ben managed to get into town and fill some drums at the petrol station.  Ellen admired the enormous living room with its beamed ceiling and polished slate floor.

'Who keeps this floor so sparkly?' she asked, 'not you surely,' she laughed knowing her friend of old, having shared a bedsit with her before she married Ben.  'You must have a good polisher.'

'Yes.  His name's Enoch.  He ties dusting pads to his feet and skates around the house to the radio putting on the polish and then shining it up.  He's a master polisher is our Enoch.  We're lucky to have him and Esta.'

The phone rang out two long blasts and one short one. Sally carried on chattering.

'Your phone's ringing, Sal. Aren't you going answer it?' asked Ellen puzzled.

'Oh no. That's not our ring,' said Sally. 'Out here we're on a party line with five of our neighbours so we have to be careful what we say on the phone,' she warned, 'but we're all very good and respect one another's privacy. Our ring is two shorts and one long by the way.'

Everything was different over here. Petrol for the lights; gas for the fridge; party lines for communication and Enoch for the cooking and polishing. It couldn't be more different from home. Ellen was enthralled by it all.

She noted the wide open stone fireplace filled with logs. Did it *really* get cold enough for a log fire? Sally assured her it did. When you were used to the heat it came as a bit of a shock when frosty nights arrived in June.

After soaking away the long journey in a soothing bath Ellen was feeling fresher in shorts and a cotton vest. She'd washed her short blond hair and left it damp to dry naturally in the warm air. It would curl, it always did, but somehow it didn't matter here. Nothing mattered very much and she was relaxing in the simplicity of it all.

The rich smell of wood smoke accompanied by an appetising aroma of cooked meat, drew her outside onto the terrace, where Ben was standing guard over a grill on top of half an oil drum. A billow of smoke rose as he used a long-handled fork to turn over juicy steaks and a ring of spicy sausage, which spat and sizzled as the juices dripped into the open fire below. Ellen had never smelt anything so good. So, this was what they meant by a braai - and as for that boerewors... mmm. Her mouth watered in anticipation.

Ben gave a piece of boerewors to each of the children who were hanging around their mother like baby elephants with their ears flapping.

'Alright now go eat your food and leave your mother in peace,' he told them firmly. They wandered off and sat on the edge of the terrace whilst Sally fired numerous questions at her friend and Ellen tried her best to answer them. How was her sister coping with her two little ones after her divorce? Were the Moors Murderers going to be hanged? Ben wanted to know about the political situation and how Britain was faring under the Labour Party. News was slow to get through from home. Long distance telephone calls had to be booked in advance and airmail letters took a while to reach far flung corners of the world. So visitors with news from home were a breath of fresh air.

After their meal Esta came to collect the children. She was little and round with cheeks as round as conkers revealing a row of perfect ivory teeth when she smiled which she appeared to do all the time. She wore a royal blue cotton smock trimmed with blue check and a little cap to match which Sally had bought for her at the local O.K. Bazaars. Sally told her she was very proud of her smart uniform. Bobbing a greeting to Ellen she held out her hand shyly and Ellen took it, charmed by the simple respectfulness of these good modest people. The children clamoured around Esta eager to tell her all their news, and she laughingly led them inside for their evening bath whilst the adults lounged in the balmy African twilight with chilled glasses of wine, chatting and listening to the pulsating chorus of cicada beetles and bullfrogs. The moon had risen and the stars of the Southern Cross were shimmering down upon them. It was another world, more basic and primitive than the one she'd left behind. Ellen was content. This was where she was meant to be.

Later that night she made her way down the long corridor in the centre of the house to the new annex which Ben had recently built. When she opened the door she screamed! There was a strange transparent creature running around on the wall next to her bed. Ellen was cowering outside the bedroom door scared to go inside when Sally came rushing up the corridor and laughed when she saw what it was.

'It's just a little gek. Nothing to be afraid of,' she chuckled, 'you'll see lots of those little lizards before you're through.  They're quite sweet really and absolutely harmless.' She touched its tail and it scuttled away into a corner.  'Don't worry.  He won't come off the wall and bite you.'  She hugged her friend, 'Goodnight, Ellen.  Sleep well.'

After watching the corner of the room for a while Ellen's eyes began to close.  She was so tired after a sleepless night on the plane that she shortly drifted off to sleep.

# Chapter 2

SHE AWOKE LATE next morning to the sun smiling through her bedroom window and the sound of children's voices outside. She got out of bed and looked out to see six year old Darren chasing five year old Gemma around the swimming pool with great glee holding a big black spider. 'Mom!' she screamed, 'tell Darren!' before jumping in the pool and laughing at him. Three year old twins Will and Sarah sat happily in the sandpit nearby - wearing armbands just in case they decided to jump in the pool. They were playing with a big fat black centipede-like creature with millions of legs. It kept curling up whenever they touched it. Laughingly Sally assured her that it was a chungululu, which, like the gek was quite harmless and the two younger children found them fascinating. Ellen shuddered. She wondered if she would ever get used to the creepy crawlies out there in the bush.

That morning during an extended breakfast, Ellen updated Sally on her break up with Eric. 'All the wedding invitations had been sent out, the church and venue were booked and he decided he didn't want to get married any more,' said Ellen, 'I never thought he would do that to me. But I suppose I'm lucky he didn't leave it till I was standing at the altar.' She smiled humourlessly.

'You poor lamb,' sympathised Sally. 'I'm sorry he treated you so badly. Believe me, Eric was no catch. You're better off without a bum like him. But his loss is my gain. Now I've got my Ellen back again.' She squeezed her friend's hand. 'At least it saved you and your parents some money. Weddings aren't cheap.'

'You're dead right Sal. How do you think I could afford to come over here?' They laughed. Sally was pleased that her friend had not retreated into her shell. It was the best thing she'd done to suggest she came over to Zambia.

That afternoon Sally took her into town in her old Ford Prefect with the four children squabbling in the back. Ellen noticed there were no new cars on the road. Most were at least eight years old. Ben had advised her to get herself a job as soon as possible so that she could register herself with the Zambian Authorities. With all the suspicion going on between Zambia and Rhodesia it was wise to have an identity card if you intended to stay for any length of time. He promised to look out for an old banger for her, just something to get her into town and back. A car was an absolute necessity.

They drove past the red tractor parked up against the hedge which Ellen had noticed the day before.

'He probably ran out of petrol,' said Sally with a grimace. 'Petrol can be expensive for the smaller farmers. If you have a truck, however decrepit, you can make a fortune transporting drums of oil from Dar es Salaam to Lusaka. Ben tells me there are abandoned trucks every few miles along the Great North Road, usually because the truck has broken down and isn't worth repairing. So they just get left on the side of the road.'

Sally checked her fuel gauge.

'That reminds me. Got to get petrol,' she said pulling into a petrol station where one lone pump was standing with a solitary African pump attendant sitting next to it on a kitchen chair waiting for customers. 'Pass me my bag please, Darren.'

She took out her purse and wound down the car window.

'Fill it up please,' she said to the hovering pump attendant, holding out some green vouchers. 'There's ten there.' The attendant grinned broadly and saluted, 'Yes ma'am.'

'What are those for?' asked Ellen intrigued.

'Oh that's part of our petrol ration for the month. All our oil is airlifted now since Britain sanctioned Rhodesia to appease the Zambians when Ian Smith refused black rule. And now the Rhodesians are getting their own back by refusing to allow oil from Mozambique through the border,' she sighed. 'They're also threatening to cut off power at the hydroelectric dam at Kariba. That wouldn't affect us of course with our generator. There are some perks to living out in the bush. It's just big boys' games,' she said despondently, 'But it's playing havoc with the economy. Farmers are battling to keep their tractors on the go. Ben works for the Farmers' Union. It's his job to go around the farms advising and servicing farming equipment but he tells me it's almost impossible sometimes without petrol. But we manage.'

They arrived at the Education Offices, a low rambling building, and parked beneath a spreading jacaranda tree on a carpet of purple blossoms. Ellen was ushered in to see Mr Mporokosa the Chief Education Officer by a tall slim woman with dark shoulder length hair, wearing horn rimmed glasses and a short floral shift. He sat in his large office overlooking the car park, cooled by an overhead fan, his vast form overflowing his chair and dwarfing his desk. Ellen took an envelope out of her bag and handed him the reference she'd been given by the headmaster of the Salford school she'd been working at for the past eighteen months. Then she gave him her teaching certificate which was still rolled up in its original cardboard tube from the University of Manchester. He studied her qualifications, asked her a few questions about her experience and nodded.

'We're badly in need of teachers with your qualifications and experience here in Zambia, Miss Sanderson,' he said in a thick Bemba accent. 'I'm prepared to offer you a contract for three years at the end of which you will be given a generous gratuity. You will find the salary compares well with the U.K. Would you like to consider before signing the contract?'

Ellen felt really excited. It had been so easy. Not like at home where she'd made an appointment to see the County's Director of Education weeks in advance. She didn't need to consider it but she needed to read the contract before signing it.

'That sounds fair,' she replied smiling.

Mr Mporokosa pressed a button on an intercom. A female voice with a South African accent answered.

'Mrs Engelbrecht, please provide Miss Sanderson with a teaching contract on her way out. And let me have a list of teaching vacancies here in Lusaka.'

Mr Mporokosa rose from his desk with amazing alacrity considering his size. He held out his hand.

'Thank you for coming in Miss Sanderson.  My secretary will look after you.'  They shook hands and Ellen left having got herself a job.

She could hardly contain her excitement when she returned to the car waving her contract.

'I can't believe it was so easy Sal.  I've got a job and I've only been here a day.'  She did a little dance before getting into the car.

Sally smiled.  She didn't tell Ellen that Ben had already put a good word in for her with the Minister of Education, who drank with him from time to time at the Lusaka Hotel.'  In that case let's go and celebrate.'

They parked in the car park of the Kawena Hills Hotel, where Sally lectured her lively brood on behaving themselves before they went in.  Inside they were shown to a table next to a long rectangular lily pool where Sally ordered chicken in the basket, a glass of white wine each and cool drinks for the children from one of the red fezzed waiters.

'Here's to a new beginning,' she said raising her glass when it arrived.

The place was buzzing with Expats in casual dress; men in shorts and t-shirts and women in pretty summer dresses.  African waiters in white uniforms and red fezzes skated between the tables carrying trays of chips and castle lagers aloft. It was all very relaxed and informal.

'Fancy seeing you here'. They looked up at a tall good looking man in a smart charcoal grey suit. His pristine white collar gleamed against the deep tan of his neck. Ellen felt embarrassed under his appraising look.

'Oh hello Dan,' said Sally. 'Haven't seen you for a while. How's Nichole?'

'She's well as far as I know. Haven't you heard? We're getting divorced.'

'Not again.' sympathised Sally. 'We really hoped you'd found the right one at last.' She turned to Ellen, 'Let me introduce you to a friend of ours, Daniel du Plessis. Dan this is my friend Ellen Sanderson. She's just come over from UK to teach in Lusaka.'

Daniel put out his hand, 'Pleased to meet you Miss Sanderson. I trust you're enjoying life in Lusaka.' Ellen looked into a pair of laughing brown eyes and was immediately drawn. She'd never met such a charming man. He had the sophistication of Stewart Granger and the animal magnetism of Elvis Presley.

'Be careful,' laughed Sally, 'he's dangerous when he's on the loose.'

'Well I certainly never managed to seduce you,' said Daniel playfully.

'Ha! Ben would have shot you with his catapult if you even thought about it,' laughed Sally

'Yeah. I didn't dare risk it,' joked Daniel smiling. They were obviously old friends.

They chatted for a few minutes, then Daniel left them, promising to pop over and see them one weekend.

'Have a word with Ben down at the club and we'll have a braai,' called Sally after him, 'and bring your swimming togs.'

Ellen watched him as he made his way around the pool, stopping every so often to chat to people, mostly women, who fluttered their eyelashes and hung onto his every word. Eventually he arrived at a table where a beautiful raven haired woman was sipping a glass of white wine. He leant over and kissed her on the cheek and then sat down opposite her.

Ellen sighed. She felt as if a light had been switched off. Sally saw the flush on her cheeks and grinned.

'He has that effect on women from nine to ninety. Don't fall for him for God's sake. He should come with a health warning. Been married twice and it looks like he's on the prowl for wife number three. Fortunately I'm immune.' She laughed and tucked into her chicken and chips.

'Mmmm. He's a bit gorgeous,' murmured Ellen. 'Is he often here?'

'Oh yes. He manages this place. Came up from Rhodesia ten years ago after his parents were killed in a road accident. No-one quite knows what happened. He doesn't talk about it. They had a farm outside Salisbury. From all accounts they left him and his sister quite a bit of money. If he's not here he's at the sports club organising events there. He likes to be in control does our Daniel. And he's very good at it. But I meant it when I said be careful. He's broken lots of hearts in this town.'

The kids were getting restless so they finished their meal and headed for the car park. But Ellen couldn't put the charismatic Daniel du Plessis out of her mind. Lusaka was becoming more and more attractive by the day.

# Chapter 3

CHRISTMAS WAS COMING and the temperatures were rising. They were now in the mid-thirties. Much of Ellen's time was spent lounging by the pool or meeting Sally and Ben's neighbours who lived on smallholdings nearby. Most of the conversation concentrated on the political situation and whether Ian Smith would eventually buckle under and give way to majority rule. The Zambian Mail made much of the fact that British troops were now in Lusaka ready to defend Zambia's borders against the well trained Rhodesian air force, but according to Ben, far from being on standby the soldiers and airmen seemed to be making good use of the bars and clubs around the town. The festive season was upon them and visitors dropped by with presents for the children, stopping off for a festive drink and a mince pie.

On Christmas Eve Ben dug up a huge fir tree from the kopje and brought it inside. He planted it in an empty oil drum and put it in the corner of the big lounge whilst they listened to Christmas carols on the transistor radio. As soft candlelight flickered on the walls they all took it in turns to hang decorations on the tree. It was how Christmas should be, thought Ellen. No commercialisation; simply children, Christmas carols and a real tree decorated on Christmas Eve. Magical.

'Hello, we have a visitor?' said Sally spotting car lights bobbing up and down on the track coming towards the house. A horn pipped as a jeep drew up outside. Ben went out to greet the visitor and came back in with Daniel du Plessis carrying an OK Bazaars bag full of presents.

'Look what the wind's blown in,' boomed Ben jovially.

'Merry Christmas Everyone,' shouted Daniel. 'Kids, I met Father Christmas on my way here. He gave me these. Put them under the tree for tomorrow morning.' He laughed, visibly enjoying the children's excitement as he doled out their presents. Ellen couldn't help thinking what a wonderful father he'd make. She wondered if either of his wives had given him children. He was a natural father.

'That's really kind of you Dan,' said Sally giving him a hug, 'don't forget to say thank you to Uncle Dan, kids so he can tell Father Christmas on his way home.' She turned to Daniel 'Now what can we get you to drink?'

'I'll have a vodka and tonic thanks,' said Dan. He turned his warm brown eyes to Ellen who was trying hard not to show that her heart was beating like a tom tom but she couldn't stop the flush rising on her cheeks.

'So, what do you think of our big metropolis, Ellen?' he asked. He had a knack of making a woman feel she was the only one in the room.

'Quite different from back home. I love everything about it,' she replied breathlessly 'the sunshine, the laid-back lifestyle, the simplicity of the local people. And I have a job starting in the New Year

'That's wonderful,' Dan drawled looking over his drink at her with simmering brown eyes. 'So you're staying then?'

'It looks like it,' smiled Ellen.

'So what's brought you away from the bright lights of the Kawena Hills Hotel?' asked Ben. 'We don't often see you out here in the sticks.'

'Well,' replied Dan, looking at Ellen, 'a group of us are going on a camping trip down the Zambezi between Christmas and New Year and I wondered if you might like to join us, Ellen. It'll be nothing fancy. There'll be about half a dozen of us and we'll be sleeping under the stars for a couple of nights and doing a bit of boating. Dirk's taking his power boat. It'll be an experience for you.' He smiled at her and his eyes danced wickedly when he saw her doubtful expression, 'No funny business, I promise,' he added, grinning at Sally and crossing his fingers over his heart. He was well aware of his reputation with the ladies.

Ellen blushed. The thought of spending nights under the stars with Daniel du Plessis was an attractive prospect but camping on the banks of the Zambezi sounded dangerous. What about the wild animals and the chungululus?

'I'm not sure,' she said hesitantly. 'I've never been camping before. There might be lions and crocodiles...' That wasn't quite true. She'd spent two nights in a bell tent in the middle of a field in Anglesey with the girl guides, but they'd been flooded out the second night and had to take shelter in the church hall. But she wasn't going to mention that uninspiring experience to the glamorous Daniel du Plessis.

Ben snorted, 'Rubbish. You'll have an amazing time. These guys have spent their whole lives in the bush. You'll be safe with them. You must go,' encouraged Ben, 'shouldn't she, Sal?'

'Mmmm,' said Sally with a quizzical look at Daniel.

'I'll behave myself, scouts honour,' he said and saluted Sally mischievously.

'You'd better!' growled Ben.

Ellen made up her mind to brave the lions and the chungalulus. 'Ok then. It sounds exciting. When are we going?'

Arrangements were made for Daniel to pick up Ellen early on Monday morning and he left amidst a chorus of Merry Christmases and thank-yous from the children and an invitation from Ben not to leave it too long until the next time.

'Well well,' said Sally as the red rear lights bumped away down the track, 'that's interesting.' She smiled. 'Just remember what I said Ellen.' Ellen suddenly felt like one of the children. But she knew her friend was just looking out for her as she'd always done. She remembered one occasion when they'd gone to a dance at the local rugby club back home. The drunken fellow who was supposed to be driving her home had leapt up on the bar and begun to strip as his mates sang lewd rugby songs. Sally had insisted that her current boyfriend must also drive Ellen home which he did none too happily because it was out of his way. Ellen could always rely on Sally to protect her. She could be a veritable Rottweiler when aroused.

'Don't worry, Sal. I'll be careful,' but Ellen couldn't help feeling exhilarated, and it wasn't the thought of wild animals that caused her heart to quicken.

Christmas Day began at the crack of dawn with the children clamouring around the tree and opening their presents amongst whoops of delight. Daniel had spared no expense, a beautiful walking doll for Gemma, a Hornby electric train set for Darren and string puppets for the twins. He'd chosen the latest Frank Herbert thriller for Sally, a historical novel for Ben and a beautiful silk scarf in shades of blue and turquoise for Ellen. She was impressed by his thoughtfulness and wished she'd been able to repay his generosity. They played water polo in the swimming pool and sat under the shade of the thatched loggia whilst Ben enjoyed himself cooking a turkey in his new Weber barbecue. Enoch, as tall and gangly as his wife was short and plump, dressed proudly in a sparkling white bush suit for the occasion, prepared mealie pop, a sort of porridge made from maize flour which they would eat with a tomato and onion sauce, whilst Sally and Ellen prepared potato and sweetcorn salads. There was far too much to eat but Sally said they could put left overs in the fridge for any visitors who happened to drop in on Boxing Day. This Christmas was light years away from the Christmases back home. It felt a bit strange to be celebrating outdoors in the sunshine but it had its own charm and Ellen loved it, but she couldn't help thinking about her forthcoming adventure.

# Chapter 4

EARLY MONDAY MORNING Daniel, casually dressed in khaki shorts and a many pocketed bush shirt, arrived in his jeep.   When Ellen went out to meet him she was disappointed to see the dark haired beauty from the Kawena Hills sitting in the cab.   Nevertheless she put on a smile as Daniel helped her to climb in next to her.  He was obviously entranced by this slim sleek haired woman who looked like she'd stepped off the catwalk even in her shorts, which displayed long tanned legs.  Next to her Ellen became very conscious of her undisciplined bouncing blond curls and plump thighs.

The girl smiled broadly revealing beautiful even white teeth.  'Hi, my name's Joanne, nice to meet you,' she said, her silver bangles jingling as she held out a slim tanned hand. Was there anything about this girl that wasn't perfect?  Ellen gave up.  There was no contest.

'Meet my sister,' said Daniel leaping up behind the wheel. He grinned when he saw the look of surprise on Ellen's face.

Maybe there was hope after all, thought Ellen. Looking at the two of them more closely she could now see the likeness. Both were long limbed with clean cut features, brown eyes and dark shiny hair. They seemed very close and got on really well judging from the fond repartee between the two of them. Daniel was obviously the adored big brother. Joanne was telling her about an incident with a huge sharp tooth barbel fish the last time they went on the river, using her hands to emphasise how big it was. Ellen noticed there were no rings on her left hand so she was seemingly unattached which seemed strange considering she was such an attractive vivacious girl. Maybe there'd been an unhappy love affair, something they might have in common. She decided to find out more as they got to know one another on this trip.

They travelled out of town for nearly two hours and then went off road until they came to the river. It was wide and grey and fast flowing with fever trees hugging the banks. They passed a pod of hippos basking in the shallows but kept on driving along the rough track beside the river until they came to a clearing where two more land rovers were parked, one with a large motor cruiser hitched to the back with *Bezi Belle* written on the side. There were two more men and another girl called Shona. Joanne got down and introduced Ellen.

'This is Shona and Manny. They're up from Rhodesia for the weekend. We've known them forever. Manny will probably spend all day fishing and Shona likes to sketch. And the unshaven hobo over there unhitching his boat is Dirk Obelheister.' She pointed to the bulky, serious looking guy wearing sun bleached blue shorts and a scruffy grey t-shirt that had once been white. 'He and Dan were at school together. He's like another big brother, always there when I need him.' Dirk looked up and nodded sombrely then returned to his task. Once the introductions were made the girls set about unpacking sleeping bags and groundsheets whilst the men launched the boat into the water.

Shona, took some beers out of a cool bag and handed them round. Ellen wasn't a beer drinker but it was hot in the midday sun and the icy metallic liquid had never tasted so good.

'Have you brought a hat?' asked Shona. Ellen shook her head. 'You'll need one if you go out on the river.' Shona fished in her bag. 'Here, use this. You don't want to get sunstroke.' She handed Ellen a beige floppy hat. 'I've got another somewhere.' They were all so friendly and generous thought Ellen. It must be the relaxed lifestyle they'd grown up with.

'Right' said Dirk jumping into the *Bezi Belle*, 'who's coming for a ride on the river?'

'How about it, Ellen?' asked Dan. 'Let's show you our great Zambezi.'

'Shona and I will stay behind and get some food on the go and Manny wants to go upstream and do some fishing,' said Joanne. She was obviously a leader and an organiser like her brother. 'See you later Big Bro. Have fun.' Ellen saw a brief look of disappointment flash across Dirk's face before he turned away and looked upriver.

Daniel helped Ellen into the boat then Dirk manoeuvred the powerful motor cruiser into mid-stream and turned her nose towards the oncoming current. They set off upstream happily viewing herds of elephant of various sizes with swinging trunks and flapping ears and hundreds of buffalo with twitching tails and bovine stares, all grazing innocently side by side on the vast stretch of grassland next to the river. At one point they stopped the boat and waited whilst a family of around twenty elephants swam across from one side of the river to the other in front of them. A black and white fish eagle landed on a tree stump sticking up at the edge of the river. It sat still for a few minutes scanning the water and then flew off as the engine started up again. Daniel pointed out colourful birdlife flitting amongst the trees, brilliant red cardinals, elegant crowned hoopoes, little yellow weavers and top heavy hornbills. Grey crocodiles camouflaged against the muddy banks hid in the shadows awaiting unsuspecting prey.

Dirk didn't speak much. He held his bottle of castle beer close to his chest in his left hand whilst steering the boat with his right. The wind ruffled the wisps of sun-bleached hair escaping from beneath his cap as he stared resolutely ahead immersed in his own thoughts.

They must have been travelling for an hour or so when disaster struck. There was a grating sound; the boat slid to a standstill and the motor cut out. They were stuck on a sandbank in the middle of the river.

'Out we get,' shouted Daniel, 'no, not you Ellen. You just keep an eye on that old bastard over there. Let us know what he's doing.'

Ellen looked downriver and saw a pod of female hippos with their babies wallowing in the shallows. Swimming around them in ever increasing circles was an enormous sentinel hippo guarding his offspring.

Whilst Dirk and Daniel pushed with all their strength to release the boat the hippo broke its circuit and began swimming purposefully towards them. They had to get away quick or his enormous jaws would be the end of them all.

Closer and closer he came, his speed belying his bulky frame. There was no denying the evil intent in his piggy eyes.

'Dirk, Daniel, he's getting out of the water!' Ellen screamed. 'Oh my God. Get us out of here, quick!' She was terrified.

The boys gave one last mighty shove and the boat was free. Jumping in smartly Dirk turned the starter key and opened the throttle.

'Go, go, go!' shouted Daniel as they sped away leaving the hippo standing on the sand bank roaring angrily after them. For a few minutes no-one spoke. They were all breathing a huge sigh of relief, and were about to congratulate themselves on getting away when Dirk groaned loudly.

'Oh hell! We're taking in water, Dan. Must've caught a rock!' He snatched off his cap and began bailing out for all he was worth, but as fast as it went out the water came back in. Soon it was covering their feet.

'Grab all the towels and plug the hole,' shouted Daniel. He grabbed his own cap from his head and shoved it at Ellen, 'Here, start bailing.' He knew it was pointless but it would give her something positive to do.

By now the murky grey water was swirling up to their ankles. An empty beer can and a yellow plastic bottle of suntan lotion bobbed around on the surface. Ellen sat on the side furiously bailing out water as Dirk and Daniel fished around feeling for their towels and trying desperately to plug the hole.

The repair lasted only a few minutes before the towels were sodden and the water was creeping up to their calves.

'We're going to sink,' shouted Dirk. 'We'll have to swim!'

Terror stricken Ellen eyed the fast flowing river, 'I'm not strong enough to swim in this,' she sobbed.

Daniel disappeared inside the cabin and came out with a life jacket. 'Here, put this on.' He thrust the jacket at her. 'That'll keep you afloat. If you lose us just let the current carry you. It'll deposit you further downstream on a bend. Just keep an eye out for crocs.'

Ellen hurriedly donned the life jacket and Daniel grabbed her hand. They all jumped overboard and were immediately swept away from the '*Bezi Belle*' which gradually sank below the surface. The water was cold despite the hot sun. Ellen held onto Daniel's hand, too scared to let go.

'I'm getting dragged under,' spluttered Daniel. 'If I don't let go I'll pull you under too.' Suddenly Ellen was on her own bobbing down river whilst Daniel receded into the distance, she couldn't see Dirk at all. The thunderous sound of Victoria Falls grew louder and louder and she panicked picturing herself being swept over into the abyss. She tried in vain to swim towards the shore but the current was too strong so she gave in and fearfully watched the banks of the river for crocodiles as she was swept remorselessly downstream…

Meanwhile Daniel and Dirk scrambled onto the bank. They were both strong swimmers having competed against each other in fast flowing rivers when they were boys.

'We've got to find Ellen, and fast,' shouted Dan anxiously. How had he managed to let her go? He'd never forgive himself if anything happened to her.

They ran along the river bank until they spotted a cabin cruiser bobbing around in the shallows.

'Anyone at home?' shouted Dirk banging on the side of the boat. 'We have an emergency.' A few minutes later a bleary eyed dishevelled figure with a weather beaten face as brown as a walnut poked his head out of the cabin looking as though he'd just woken up.

'Hello there. What's wrong?'

'We need your boat urgently. My boat is wrecked and a friend is out there in the river.'

'Jump in,' he shouted, suddenly wide awake, 'Let's go.' Within seconds they were speeding along the river, scanning the water and the banks intently for signs of Ellen.

They scoured the wide grey river for a couple of miles and Daniel was becoming more and more fraught. Where was she? Had she managed to get ashore, and if so where?

'We'll try one more time,' frowned Dirk, 'We need to find her before it gets dark and the hippos come out of the water.'

The river swept around a bend and Ellen found herself close to the bank. She grabbed an overhanging branch and held on for dear life as the water rushed by. Oh God, was that a croc sliding into the water? He'd lain there invisible against the muddy bank and now crawled determinedly towards her. Her arms ached but she frantically hauled herself along the branch and managed to climb up into the safety of the tree, exhausted.

She was amazed at how she'd dealt with it all but having no choice she'd had to face up to the challenge of staying alive, and she'd done it, all on her own. She wasn't naturally courageous, the opposite in fact. As one of the youngest of a family of six she'd never been a leader, had never been one to break the rules. But here she was, sitting on a branch looking down at a crocodile in the Zambezi River. It was so ridiculous she almost laughed out loud. The folks back home would never believe it. Dirk and Daniel were nowhere to be seen. She was alone now but amazingly she felt quite calm. The river had done its worst. She'd faced hippos and crocs and the wrath of the mighty Zambezi. Nothing could scare her now, and she was confident the boys would find a way of coming to rescue her.

She just hoped it would be soon.

# Chapter 5

THE AFTERNOON WORE on and Ellen felt as if she'd been in the tree for days rather than hours. She was getting worried thinking she might never be found. It was going to be dark soon and she was terrified of climbing down from the tree and hiking through the bush in case there was something on the ground ready to devour her. After what seemed like an eternity she thought she heard the sound of an engine in the distance, she strained to hear it and moved along the branch closer to the river, but she couldn't move too far in case the branch bowed and tipped her into the water. That croc might still be lying in wait. Yes, she was sure. Somewhere further upstream there was a motor boat. The sound grew louder as it came towards her. She had to find a way of attracting its attention. She struggled out of her shirt and shorts whilst holding on to the branch with one hand, and waited until the boat was nearly abreast of the tree, then she let them go one after the other and shouted for all she was worth.

'Help! Help!' The shorts had landed on another branch of the tree and stayed there but the shirt fell into the river and floated out next to the boat. At first she thought they hadn't heard her over the noise of the engine but then whoever was on board saw the shirt billowing in the water and stopped the engine.

'Help me! I'm up here!' The engine started again and the boat nosed towards the bank. It came to a stop under the tree.

'I'm up here,' shouted Ellen. A face looked up and Ellen recognised the familiar dancing brown eyes of Daniel du Plessis.

'What on earth are you doing up there in your bra and pants?' laughed Daniel.

Ellen was furious. How could he joke at a time like this? 'Don't just stand there laughing,' she shouted angrily. She was beyond joking 'Get me down right now.'

An hour later they were back at the campsite and Ellen had calmed down, although she was still not happy with Daniel, first for letting go of her hand and then for laughing at her predicament. She sat next to the campfire feeling embarrassed and clutching a towel around her whilst Joanne rummaged in the back of the jeep for a spare pair of trousers and a t-shirt.

That evening they had cause to rejoice and there was much hilarity. Rik, the owner of the rescue boat was invited to join the party. It turned out he was a game warden on a weekend's leave and he entertained them with his stories of close encounters with the Big Five. Wine corks popped and the store of beers in the back of Daniel's jeep gradually diminished as the party celebrated well into the night, until everyone, especially Daniel, was well and truly oiled. He'd also entertained his audience telling jokes and doing a tribal dance around the campfire until, exhausted, he fell down in a heap next to Ellen and fell asleep.

Joanne came and sat next to her, 'As you can see my brother enjoys a party,' she laughed. 'He's having a tough time at the moment with this divorce. It's good to see him relaxing.'

'Did they have any children?' asked Ellen.

'Good heavens no. They were only married for a year and Nichole was too worried about her figure to fall pregnant, but she's taking him to the cleaners with the divorce settlement. The last one walked away with a nice little packet too. All his money has gone. I just wish he'd meet someone who'll love him for himself and not what she can get out of him. He'd love kids though. Just hasn't found the right one.'

Ellen looked down at Daniel sleeping innocently in the firelight and felt a moment of tenderness recalling how excited he'd been handing out presents to Sally's children on Christmas Eve. She could imagine him with a household of kids. He was a big kid himself really. She suddenly had an anxious thought, 'Will there be anyone staying awake tonight?' She was nervous about wild animals roaming into their camp.

'Don't worry. Dirk sleeps with his rifle cocked and one eye open. He was brought up in the bush. He and Dan usually take it in turns to keep watch. And anyway the herds of buck and zebra are much further upstream where it's more open. That's where the predators hunt, where there's food. These boys know where it's safe to stop. Dan and Dirk used to be off camping every weekend when we were kids.'

'It's a shame about Dirk's boat. Do you think they'll be able to salvage it?'

Joanne shrugged. 'Who knows? But Dirk will have it well insured. He's a big shot in Sunlife. He won't lose out.'

Ellen looked at Daniel next to her and smiled, 'I don't think there's much chance of Daniel being on guard tonight.'

'No,' agreed his sister smiling indulgently. 'But I think he's deserved his sleep tonight, don't you? Don't worry, Dirk will make sure we're safe. I'd trust him with my life.'

They were silent for a moment lulled by the firelight and the wine.

'How about you and Dirk?' asked Ellen? 'Anything going on there with you two?' Joanne laughed.

'Good heavens no. Dirk's just a friend. I work for him and I've known him ever since we were kids.' She paused and looked pensively out at the river, 'but there was someone once, a long time ago now. His name was Josh. We were going to be married,' her face saddened.

'So what happened?'

'It's a long story. One day I'll tell you all about it. But now I'm going to turn in.' She stood up. 'See you in the morning Ellen. And I'm glad Dan invited you along.' She bent down and pecked Ellen on the cheek,' I reckon you and I are going to be good friends.'

One by one they crawled into their sleeping bags except for Dirk who sat with his back against a tree, his rifle by his side. Ellen draped a blanket over Daniel, not that it was cold, just because she felt protective. She left him by the fire before creeping into her own bed. She tossed and turned until, nervously, she gathered up her sleeping bag and took it over to lie beside him at the campfire. For some reason next to him she felt safe and was soon fast asleep.

The following day they awoke late. After a huge fry up on the campfire Daniel suggested they should all go for a walk through the bush? He knew of a special place he wanted to show Ellen.

'I want to make up for yesterday,' he said apologetically.

'Oh yes. You'll love it Ellen,' exclaimed Joanne full of enthusiasm.

Daniel put his finger to his lips, 'sh! Sis, don't spoil the surprise.'

The others elected to stay behind. Manny wanted to do some more fishing and Shona already had her sketch pad out and was working on a sketch of the campfire she'd started the night before. Dirk had seen it all before and without his boat he was lost, so he accepted an invitation from Rik to spend the morning with him on the river. He wanted to go and find the spot his boat went down. If it wasn't too deep maybe it could be salvaged.

Ellen and Joanne followed Daniel who carried a rifle over his shoulder just in case. They walked silently in single file down the river bank and then after about half a mile he turned away from the river along a sandy trail. They came to a pile of dung on the path. He crouched down to look more closely and stuck his index finger into it.

'You can't be serious,' cried Ellen wrinkling her nose in disgust and Joanne chuckled.

'This is elephant droppings,' he informed Ellen. 'A herd came along here quite recently.'

'How can you tell?' asked Ellen, still disgusted by the sight of Daniel sticking his finger into the poo.

'It's still warm,' he replied with amusement.

'Just keep your hands to yourself now till you've disinfected them,' she said warily.

They rounded a clump of trees and ahead there was a large waterhole.

'Get down and stay very quiet,' whispered Daniel. They all sat down next to a bush and waited.

After twenty silent minutes of sitting there without shade in the heat of the day Ellen was getting restless. What were they waiting for? But then she held her breath as the spectacle unfolded before them. Emerging stealthily from behind the trees, came a great bull elephant, his huge ears flapping like sails cooling him from the hot sun. He lifted his sensitive trunk high in the air and sniffed, then slowly lumbered towards the waterhole, his superb white tusks resplendent in the sunlight. Behind him came more bulls of various sizes.   They gathered around the pool as if in conference sucking up the water with their supple leathery trunks.  When they'd had their fill they slowly melted away making way for the female elephants and their young. Matriarchs rumbled greetings to their sisters and gently nudged their young offspring forward to the water's edge, whilst aunts chastised troublesome teenagers and trumpeted warnings when they pushed and misbehaved.  Tiny babies with miniature trunks on wobbly legs, played around their mother's legs in the muddy water.  Ellen was enchanted. The scene lasted half an hour and then they had gone leaving the waterhole serene and ripple free again.

Without a word they rose, brushed the sand off their shorts and returned to the camp.  There were no words to describe what had just taken place but Ellen was full of gratitude to Daniel for showing her this magical sight.

The next day was Sunday and they all had to get home for work the following day.  They packed up camp after lunch and said goodbye to Manny and Shona who were returning to Salisbury.  Dirk was eager to get back to Lusaka to inform the insurance company about the loss of his boat. He and Rik had found the place where it went down and he'd dived down to investigate.  He hoped it could be raised and the hole in the bow mended, although he didn't seem too worried.  Nothing seemed to worry Dirk.  Joanne told her he had another little putt putt motor boat which he kept down at Kariba but he liked something more powerful to take on river trips. Ellen had tried to make conversation with him over the weekend but found him taciturn and uninformative so she gave up. Joanne and Daniel seemed to be the only ones he communicated with.

The journey back to Lusaka was uneventful. After the first half hour of chatter the girls fell asleep leaving Daniel to his own thoughts. Ellen wasn't his usual choice in women. He normally went for slim brunettes with silky tresses and long tanned legs. His last two wives were both very attractive trophies but they had no depth and they were demanding. Oh how demanding. Nichole had driven him crazy with her carping on about buying a big house in Cape Town. Why go and live in Cape Town when he had everything he needed here? His first wife Lisa was jealous and possessive and she'd suffocated him with her constant demands. But there was something about Ellen. She was different. She had depth and pluck. Look at the way she'd kept her head on the river. Lisa would have been hysterical, Nichole wouldn't even have bothered to go out in the boat at all. She was too worried about her looks to go where her hair would be blown out of place. Ellen on the other hand was independent, intelligent and caring and she wasn't afraid to speak her mind. He found her a breath of fresh air, and most important of all he felt at ease with her. Although he wouldn't admit it he'd felt a warmness when he'd woken up the other morning, which wasn't only due to the blanket Ellen had thrown over him. He wanted to get to know her better, but he had a problem, a problem that was only just beginning to reveal itself to him and which he justified to himself whenever he thought about it. His job required him to be the life and soul of the party, to be the host, ever ready to entertain. Very few people knew the sensitive man hidden beneath the outgoing personality he portrayed to the world fuelled by booze and poker. The façade was becoming harder to keep up. He needed to find out if Ellen would be happy with the real Daniel, the one he hid from the rest of the world.

# Chapter 6

BACK IN LUSAKA Ellen got stuck into her new teaching position. She'd been posted to Lusaka Girls' School which gave her the option of living in the boarding hostel next to the school. She was enjoying her job far more than she'd ever done before. Her class of twelve year old girls consisted of the daughters of Government Minister's with a smattering of European children from outlying farms who boarded at the hostel along with pupils from the neighbouring Boys' School.

Staying out of town with Sally and Ben had been fun but not practical. Ben was on the lookout for a suitable old banger he could do up for her but hadn't yet managed to find one. With no car Ellen had to rely on Sally ferrying her twelve miles in and out of town every day, which was alright going into town as she had to take the children to the infant school each day. Dropping Ellen off at the Girls' School in the morning wasn't a problem. Bringing her home was more difficult. On three days a week the children and Ellen all finished school at 1pm, but on the other two days she had to do afternoon school which meant that Sally had to make a special journey to collect her. With rationing they had to conserve petrol, so Ellen had chosen to live in the Hostel next door to the school where there was always the company of other young teachers out on contract. Like her they were enthusiastic to explore their new surroundings, so for the first few weeks she had little time to think of anything other than preparing lessons and getting to know her colleagues. She took her turn on hostel duty at the weekends when she walked the children to church, supervised their homework and kept an eye on them down at the pool, not to mention hilarious fancy dress parties and trips over to braai with Sally and Ben. Life sparkled and she loved it.

Teaching was a joy. The children were disciplined and respectful. They were enthusiastic to learn which in turn made her enthusiastic to teach them. One morning after a particularly late night when she and her hostel buddies had talked over coffee early into the following morning, she overslept and was awoken by a knock on her door.

'Ellen it's gone eight. Time you weren't here.' It was the hostel matron Mrs Motherwell who kept a motherly eye on children and teachers alike.

Hurriedly she dressed, skipped breakfast and ran the short distance through the trees to the school, jacaranda pods popping under her feet as she went. She was sure that she was in for a good ticking off from Mrs Jessop, the headmistress who always reminded her of the Yorkshire terrier her parents used to have, small and yappy with a bark much worse than her bite.

She headed down the quiet corridors towards her classroom at the end of the building, suspecting that the principal had already gone in to quell any noise. Hesitating at her classroom door, she struggled to think of a good excuse, but could think of none, so she took a deep breath and walked in. The children's heads were all bent over their desks hard at work on a task she had set them the day before.

'Has anyone been in to supervise you?' she asked, astonished at their self-discipline. They looked at her with big brown eyes and shook their heads innocently. It was unbelievable. At home there would have been a riot going on. Once again Ellen couldn't believe how easy life was in that part of the world.

Her work life wasn't the only thing that had improved. Her social life was also better than it had ever been. One evening at the Hostel they were all sitting around chatting after dinner in the hostel lounge when Mick, one of the teachers from the Boys' School, had a suggestion. He was a vibrant character with a shock of brown hair which continually flopped over his eyes. There was something about Mick's eyes which Ellen couldn't quite put her finger on. Then it hit her. He had one brown eye and one blue one which was strangely attractive. He was always coming up with something different for them to do.

'There's a badminton court laid out in the gym at my school which no-one uses. How about we go over and use it?'

'What about racquets?' asked Ellen? She had a tennis racquet and was a pretty good hitter on the tennis court but had never played badminton before.

'There's a few spares in the games cupboard. We can use those until we have our own.'

So the following Tuesday they all met outside the Boys' School in their tennis gear at the other end of the playing field whilst Mick opened up the school gym and doled out racquets from the sports cupboard. Ellen had been into Lusaka and bought a snappy little tennis dress for the occasion which showed off her newly acquired tan and made her legs look leaner than they were, and she was feeling good about herself.

It became a regular badminton evening twice a week on Tuesdays and Thursdays. Ellen found the hitting action was different to what she was used to on the tennis court where it was a whole arm movement whereas in badminton it was a flick of the wrist, but she soon got used to it. Mick organised home tournaments and soon they were good enough to form a team. Ellen hadn't enjoyed herself this much for a long time. She was having too much fun to think of Daniel du Plessis. After a while they decided it was time to join the league which eventually took them down to the sports club to play an away match.

Dripping with perspiration after a hard won game they trooped into the crowded bar for a drink where Ellen recognised Daniel's lazy drawl coming from the other side of the room. He spotted her and came across carrying his usual vodka and tonic.

'This is a pleasant surprise. Let me buy you a drink, Ellen. What are you having?'

'I'll have a rock shandy thanks,' she said, wiping her brow with her towel.

'And for your friend?'

Mick shook his head, 'Not for me thanks.'

When he'd gone off to the bar Mick grinned at her, 'He fancies you. Better watch out. I've heard stories about him.'

Then seeing Dan winding his way back with their drinks he disappeared to chat to some of his friends.

'There's a few of us going down to Kariba for the weekend,' said Daniel as he handed her a rock shandy. 'Do you fancy coming along? Joanne and Dirk will be going and Dirk has a small motor dinghy he keeps down there. I can assure you there are no fast flowing rivers or hippos and it'll be a lazy time. You'll enjoy it,' he added seeing her hesitate. It had been some time but he'd found her face kept popping into his mind.

'Oh I don't know,' said Ellen. 'I've been invited to drive to Vic Falls this weekend with a crowd of friends,' Sally had repeated her warnings relentlessly about Daniel's drinking and gambling lifestyle and she wasn't sure any more if she wanted to get involved in spite of the attraction. She'd come here to get away from a broken engagement. More man trouble was the last thing she needed.

Daniel's pride was at stake but he didn't show it. He wasn't used to women turning him down and he wasn't prepared to give up that easily.

He put on his most charming smile and touched her shoulder briefly sending a spurt of electricity coursing through her, 'Joanne's over there. Come and say hello.'

*Dammit it!* She thought, *why did he have to do that?*

She allowed him to guide her across the busy room to where his sister was chatting vivaciously to a group of people at the other side of the bar.

'Hello, Ellen. Where've you been hiding? I've missed you. Come and sit down.' Joanne pulled out a stool for her.

'Oh you know. A new job and all that. I've been settling in.' Ellen climbed onto the barstool beside her.

'Are you joining us on our trip to Kariba Lake this weekend?' she enthused, 'You'll love it. We get up late, go out in the boat, do a bit of fishing, maybe a swim, come back, read a book and then braai in the evening. Please say you'll come. I need some girl company.'

'Mmmm. Well…'

'Oh go on. You know you want to.' When Ellen hesitated she said, 'Well that's settled then. We'll pick you up around five on Friday. All you need is a bikini and a pair of shorts.'

Later whilst she was supervising the children's bedtime Ellen was annoyed with herself for allowing her arm to be twisted so easily. She kidded herself that now she was committed and couldn't let Joanne down.

They left on Friday evening and travelled for an hour along the Chirundu Road before turning off on a sand road towards Kariba. The road helter skeltered around bends on the escarpment, first uphill and then down amongst rocks and bushland. By this time it was getting dark and Daniel was using his headlights. As they rounded a sweeping bend Ellen caught her breath. There in the headlights was a magnificent male lion, his face surrounded by a great golden mane, sleeping on the warm sand by the side of the road. As they passed he looked up sleepily, his eyes like amber pools, then lowered his head onto his huge paws and continued his slumbers with not a care in the world.

'Ohhhh' she breathed. 'Did you see that?'

'Magnificent wasn't he,' murmured Daniel. 'Like all cats they like nothing better than a warm place to sleep. He'll be happy there until the sand cools and then he'll go home and see what his wife's caught for dinner.'

'Typical man,' joked Joanne, and they all laughed.

They accepted it all so casually thought Ellen but she was entranced; her first lion. He'd live in her memory forever.

# Chapter 7

DAN AND ELLEN relaxed in their swimwear under a wattle canopy sipping ice cold lagers. They gazed out over the lake at a small island which was a few hundred yards from the shore, whilst the little green motor boat they'd borrowed from Dirk bobbed up and down at the foot of the steps leading up to the lakeside motel. Daniel had been the soul of good manners and she'd found it difficult to refuse when he suggested they should leave the others sleeping off the party from the night before and go for a ride on the lake. She noticed he hadn't drunk as much as the others. Perhaps Sally was wrong about him.

Earlier he had packed a half a dozen dumpies in the ice bag and they had motored the short distance from their campsite in Siavonga to the other side of the island, hoping to find a private beach where they could swim and relax in the mid-morning sun. But all they could see there were a few straggly tree branches reaching out from the bottom of the lake, the remains of a valley where animals and people once roamed. In the other direction, at least a mile away they could see the heat hazed shores of Rhodesia. The Zambezi valley between the two countries was now flooded by the Zambezi River which had been dammed in order to produce hydro-electricity. So, finding no apparent place to land, they had remained in the boat for a while drinking ice cold lagers, then as it got hotter, they'd chugged back, stopping on the way at the motel for a drink.

'This is heaven,' sighed Ellen, stretching her tanned arms languorously above her blond curls like a cat. 'I could stay here all day. I'm glad we went out early. It would've been too hot this afternoon'.

'We can book in if you like and go back to the campsite tomorrow,' replied Dan, taking a long swig from his bottle of Castle lager. 'Separate rooms of course.' He added hastily. Ellen was amused. He was really quite a gentleman when you got to know him she thought.

'Do you think it will be O.K. to leave the boat down there overnight?' she asked.

Dan stood up and padded to the edge of the terrace in his bare feet. He looked towards the far end of Lake Kariba. A band of cloud was beginning to appear over the horizon a hundred and fifty miles away. He came back and shook his head.

'There's a storm brewing. Perhaps it would be better to come back another time. I've a feeling Dirk is planning a day's fishing tomorrow and I don't want us to get caught in a storm on the lake. The boat may get damaged if we leave it down there overnight.'

'Shame. We'd better finish our drinks then and get back,' Ellen yawned and picked up her canvas beach bag reluctantly. It had been a wonderful day and Daniel had been the perfect companion.

Dan signalled to the hovering African waiter in khaki shirt and trousers, and paid the bill. 'Bonsella' he said with a smile, handing him a generous tip, and the old man put his hands together and bowed respectfully in thanks. They were just getting up to go when there was the hum of a motor boat approaching. As it came into view they saw that it was sleek and white with a green and red Zambian flag fluttering from the prow. It parked at the landing stage dwarfing their little green boat. Out jumped a young African in a sparkling white shirt and shorts, a perfect advertisement for Persil. He ran smartly up the many steps and strode briskly towards them.

'Is that your boat down there, Sir?' he asked politely.

'Er, yes. Is there a problem?' replied Dan, uncertainly.

'I am a Republic of Zambia Customs and Immigration Officer,' he told them imperiously.   'You must both accompany me to the Police Station immediately.'

Ellen and Dan looked at each other in alarm.  What on earth had they done?  But it was best not to argue with these officials or you could be in big trouble.  So they followed him meekly down the steps and Dan helped Ellen into the boat, then hopped in athletically himself.  Their driver never said a word as he drove them along the shoreline to another set of steps which led up to a large, round thatched building perched on the headland; apparently the Siavonga  police station.  They disembarked and followed the Officer up the steps to a lawned area with a tall palm tree in the centre surrounded by colourful flowering shrubs.  A flag pole with the Zambian flag hanging limply from the top denoted its official status.  It all looked very peaceful and civilised with no sign of prison bars, so Ellen breathed a sigh of relief.  Soon they would find out what the problem was and Dan would sort it out.  Then they could return to the motel and get their boat back to the campsite in safety.

They were led inside where more white suited officials sat behind a counter.

'Names?' asked one of the officers, pen poised.

'Daniel du Plessis and Ellen Sanderson. Why have you brought us here?' asked Daniel. He had been thinking of the injustice of it all whilst in the boat, and was now indignant at the high handed way they were being treated.

'I am arresting you on the charge of entering Rhodesia illegally and spying for the Rhodesian government,' answered an older policeman, who was obviously in charge. There had been suspicion between the two countries ever since Zambian Independence when Ian Smith's Rhodesia had refused to hand over to an African government.

Daniel looked stunned. 'That's ridiculous,' he gasped. 'We're down here for a weekend's fishing from Lusaka. We've no intention of visiting Rhodesia.' His eyes went dark and his handsome face took on a stubborn look.

'You will stay here until the Chief Immigration Officer arrives from the Bridge.'

The Bridge was the road on top of the dam wall which separated Zambia from Rhodesia.

'And how long will that be?' asked Daniel still smarting from the ridiculous charge.

'We don't know. The Chief Immigration Officer is a very busy man,' replied the police officer pompously. 'Maybe half an hour, maybe an hour. In the meantime you must both wait outside.  I cannot allow you to disrespect the Police Station in a state of undress.'

Ellen and Daniel looked at one another in disbelief and a smile played on Ellen's lips as she wrapped her towel around her.  Less amused, Daniel was about to protest, but Ellen put her hand on his arm,

'Let's just wait outside, Dan.  It's not far from the Bridge. He can't be long.'

Reluctantly Daniel gave in and they both went to sit under the palm tree, which was the only place with any shade.  Fortunately they had grabbed their towels from the boat before they came, which helped to protect them from the African sun, now blazing down mercilessly from the noon day sky.  Ellen also had sun screen and a half bottle of water in her bag.

An hour later they were still there, humiliated and angry in their swimming costumes, moving around to catch the shade of the palm tree's shadow, which fortunately became larger as the afternoon wore on.  But the Chief Immigration Officer didn't appear.  They'd been there for two hours now and big black clouds were looming steadily closer.  Daniel was getting really angry.  Ignoring Ellen's warnings he stalked into the police station, incensed and ready for battle.

'There's a storm brewing,' he shouted fiercely throwing caution to the wind, 'and my boat's still moored back at the motel.   Not to mention the fact that we have been left outside in the mid-day sun without shelter for the past two hours.   I warn you, if anything happens to my boat because of this I will hold you personally responsible.'

Miraculously the attitude of the Police Officer changed. He became more respectful and eager to please.

'Just wait here a second, Sir.   I'll phone the Chief Immigration Officer now.' He disappeared into an office at the rear and came back twenty seconds later, seemingly having made a phone call but Daniel had his doubts.

'You can go now, Sir.  But you must report to the Bridge within the next two hours.  My Officer will take you back to the motel.'

Daniel took a deep breath.   It was obvious that these officers had been amusing themselves at their expense.   It was pointless to protest, but he hated the thought that they were laughing at him.

Back at the campsite they pulled their boat onto the small shingle beach in front of the open rondavels where the others were already building a fire to cook supper.

'Where have you two been?' asked Dirk with a sly grin, 'we were about to send out a search party.'

'You'd never believe it if I told you,' grumbled Daniel.

'Try us,' said Joanne winking at the others.

After he'd entertained the party with their spy story Daniel and Ellen drove up to the Bridge for their interview with the Chief Immigration Officer. Warm raindrops were beginning to tap on the jeep's canvas top as they parked in the empty car park beside the Customs post and walked into the long cool room, where the Customs Officer on duty directed them to an office at the end of a corridor.

Daniel knocked on the door and a deep voice called, 'Enter.'

The official who greeted them was a mature, stockily built man of mixed blood with a pleasant attitude. He rose from his desk, shook hands with Daniel and introduced himself as Chief Immigration Officer McKenzie. He listened to their story then took them to a large map on the wall where he showed them how the course of the Zambezi had originally meandered through the valley.

'That,' he told them, 'is the border-line between Zambia and Rhodesia,' and he traced the meandering course of the river with his finger. 'So, effectively, when you went behind that island you were in Rhodesian territory.'

Daniel nodded. 'I see. What will happen now?'

The Officer looked at the young couple and smiled sympathetically. He knew the tricks the younger officers played on visitors. It got pretty boring up at that police station on the headland. He could remember a time not so long ago when all this uncertainty and suspicion between the two Rhodesias hadn't existed and he was becoming bored with all the suspicion and subterfuge. One of these days he dreamed of buying himself a little inn out in the countryside where he would enjoy playing host to decent people whose only intent was to get away from all this political nonsense. They were fortunate to live in one of the most beautiful countries in the world. All most people wanted was to live in it peacefully together.

'This time we'll let you off with a caution,' he said kindly, 'but next time it would be wise to study a map of the lake before you venture out in your boat. It's easy to be confused and you might not be so lucky in future,' he warned ominously.

'Thank you,' said Daniel gratefully, 'It won't happen again.' He was annoyed with himself for not knowing that. He should have known better but he wasn't about to admit it. Sometimes it was best to plead ignorance. Now that was over he looked forward to a relaxing day's tiger fishing on the lake followed by an evening by the campfire with good friends, a glass of wine and Ellen who seemed to be softening towards him after her initial hesitation.

Ellen breathed a sigh of relief. She wouldn't be seeing the inside of a Zambian gaol. Not this time anyway. Everything seemed to happen when she was with Daniel du Plessis. He seemed to attract trouble but he also attracted her! Life was never this exciting with Eric back in the drizzle of Manchester. The sun, the exotic surroundings and Daniel du Plessis were a dangerous cocktail which was becoming harder to resist.

# Chapter 8

IN THE FOLLOWING months Ellen spent a lot of time down at the Sports Club. She helped serve hotpot suppers to the cricketers on match days and helped out at the Casino nights which Daniel liked to organise. She found gambling boring but she was prepared to make a show of enjoying herself just to please him. During weekdays she would join him for lunch down at the Hotel next to the lily pool where the African staff now referred to her as 'Mrs du Plessis'. Weekends were spent at Kariba or sometimes during her school holidays she would accompany him on his trips around the country visiting other hotels in the Kawena Hills Group. She loved it when she went with him to Livingstone where the mist of Victoria Falls could be seen from miles away. On those occasions they would drive down the road to the great waterfall, sit and have a drink at the café, laugh at the antics of the baboons and watch mesmerised whilst the torrents of water thundered over into the gorge below sending up a curtain of spray which absorbed the sun and produced a magnificent rainbow.  No wonder it was called 'the smoke that thunders,' thought Ellen, or Mosi-oa-Tunya as the Africans christened it.  It was such a poetic turn of phrase.

Back home after an evening's socialising at the club when neither of them were on duty, they would go back to Daniel's house where they would lie quietly next to the pool whispering their secrets and staring into each other's eyes, making love under the warm night sky.  Unless she was on duty at the hostel, Ellen now spent most of her nights with Daniel at his rented house next door to the hotel.  They were spending every moment they could together and Ellen was falling helplessly in love.  There was always something exciting going on when he was around.  She'd never felt as alive as when she was with Daniel du Plessis and she would drop everything to be with him.  She even gave up her badminton against the advice of Ben who could see that she was gradually losing her identity to Daniel, so total was her obsession.  But the feelings were mutual.  Daniel too felt happier than he'd been for a long time.  Sally of course continued to warn her that Daniel drank too much and gambled too freely but her heart won over her head and all common sense flew out of the window.  She couldn't see what the problem was, so Sally shook her head wearily and said nothing more about it.  Ellen was sure that it was simply the job that made him drink so much, and anyway, he was no different to everyone else. Everyone drank in Lusaka, so she put any concerns to the back of her mind.

By the following September Daniel's divorce was almost complete. Nichole had demanded a large settlement but he felt it was worth it to be free of her. She was now living down in Cape Town having hooked herself a millionaire playboy, but good luck to her was all Daniel would say of his ex-wife. He never bad mouthed his ex-wives. All he wanted was to be with Ellen.

One balmy evening whilst they sat at the poolside Daniel suddenly jumped up and disappeared into the house. Ellen lay back on the lounger looking up into the star speckled sky with its huge pendulous moon. She breathed in the scent of the honeysuckle winding through the breeze block pool enclosure and was aware of the happy laughter sounds wafting over from around the lily pool next door. She was so happy it scared her. No one had the right to be as happy as she was. The bubble had to break sometime. Daniel appeared above her with a bottle and two champagne flutes. She sat up and trailed her feet over the edge of the lounger into the pool.

'What are we celebrating?' she asked, her heart beating fast in anticipation.

He sat down beside her and handed her a glass. In the bottom there was a beautiful sapphire and diamond ring.

'I love you Ellen and I want you to marry me.' Fleetingly Sally's warnings crossed her mind but she dismissed them. She wasn't going to let anything spoil this blissful romantic moment. Once Daniel had settled down to married life she was sure he would lay off the booze and the gambling. She loved him so much he would change. She knew he would.

'I thought you'd never ask.' she said, kissing him and admiring the beautiful ring he placed on her finger. As if on tap the strains of *Strangers in the Night* floated over from the hotel.

'Come and dance with me,' said Daniel. He took her in his arms and they swayed to the music. Ellen felt as if she'd come home.

# Chapter 9

THEY MARRIED IN October at the registry office down the road from the hotel. It was arranged very quickly, as soon as Daniel's divorce came through. Daniel had tried to get a church wedding but because he'd been divorced none of the clergy would do it. Ellen would have liked to have swept down the aisle in a white dress surrounded by her friends and family, but it wasn't going to happen so she accepted it. Marrying Daniel was more important to her than anything else wherever the wedding took place. There was no need for a big occasion seeing as neither had family to invite, apart from Joanne who was just pleased to see her brother happy and finally marrying someone she approved of. Joanne and Dan's parents had been killed in a nasty road accident ten years before in Rhodesia. When Ellen expressed sympathy and asked what had happened neither seemed willing to talk about it so she asked no further questions not wishing to cause them unnecessary pain. Ellen's parents couldn't be there either because her father was ill and the journey would be too much for him, and the rest of her family couldn't afford the air fare, so it was only Joanne, Dirk, Sally and Ben they needed to invite. The rest were friends and colleagues.

Ellen had run up her own mini skirted wedding dress on the hostel sewing machine from some material she'd been meaning to make into a tennis dress, whilst Daniel's suit was made in a rush by an Indian tailor and had one sleeve longer than the other.

On the day of the wedding Ben picked Ellen up from the hostel and they drove in his Rover to the registry office expecting Daniel to be waiting there. It was seven minutes to twelve and they'd been told not to be late because there was another wedding at 12.30 but Daniel and Dirk were nowhere to be seen.

Meanwhile at the hotel Dirk parked his Mercedes outside the entrance and prepared to do his best man duty making sure his friend was ready. He'd done this twice before; it was becoming a habit and he hoped this would be third time lucky. Of all Daniel's friends Dirk knew him best. He knew all about his bad habits, his excessive drinking and gambling. Since their school days they'd shared many a drunken evening, many hands of poker and he'd listened patiently to all Dan's marital problems. But they couldn't be more different in temperament which was probably why they remained such good friends. Daniel enjoyed the limelight. He was an entertainer and an organiser which is why he sparkled in the hotel business where his customers adored him. To begin with it had been natural for him but the stress of having to be continually entertaining was taking its toll and he had become more reliant on alcohol to keep him going. On the other hand Dirk liked a drink but he didn't rely on it. He had always been retiring and reliable. Many a time he'd had to extricate his friend from sticky situations. He'd forgotten the number of times he'd lied to protect him. After he left school he'd started out as an insurance salesman in Southern Rhodesia. That was fifteen years ago and over the years his superiors had recognised his potential as a negotiator. Climbing the ladder of success he now controlled the whole of Sunlife's Central African territory which covered Rhodesia, Zambia, Tanzania and Uganda. Dirk had never had an outgoing personality. He was reserved and uncommunicative with strangers, only relaxing with people he knew well, but once he put on the Sunlife mantle he became confident and in command.

He knew where he would find Dan and walked straight into the bar to find his friend slouched on a stool on his second vodka.

'Are you ready pal,' he asked. 'It's almost time.'

'Just finishing this then we can go,' said Dan. 'Have you got the ring?'

Dirk opened his jacket and put his hand into the inside pocket. 'Oh hell! It's gone,' he teased. He said this every time so Daniel just grinned.

'Come on, then let's get going,' he said throwing back the remains of his vodka, 'I mustn't be late for Ellen.'

They climbed into the white merc and Dirk turned the key. There was a grinding sound but the car didn't start. He tried again, nothing.

'Bugger it!' exploded Dirk. 'The damn battery has died. We'll have to take your jeep Dan.'

'It's round at the house next door.' Daniel looked at his watch. 'It's nearly ten to twelve. Ellen will be there in two minutes. We were told not to be late by the registrar.'

'If you hadn't had that last drink we'd have had loads of time,' grumbled Dirk. 'Come on. We'll just get round there if we run. Let's hope Ellen's late.' They set off running down the hotel driveway.

Ellen was beginning to feel foolish. Daniel should be there already. What had happened to him? Dirk was supposed to have picked him up at quarter to twelve. He should have been there waiting for her. Everyone else was there. What would they be thinking?

'Don't worry,' said Ben calmly, seeing her embarrassment. 'We'll just drive around the block. He'll be here when we get back.' After their second circuit with no sign of her groom Ellen was getting annoyed and was ready to cancel the wedding, but Ben insisted on trying one more time.

When they arrived back at the entrance the third time Daniel was getting out of his jeep followed by his best man, Dirk.

'Don't blame Dan,' pleaded Dirk seeing the frown on Ellen's face. 'My car wouldn't start and we had to run around to the house for Dan's car.' Ellen was mollified. It couldn't be helped but everything would be alright now. They crowded inside the small room, Joanne and Sally who were there as witnesses, Mick who was taking photos with an instamatic camera, the crowd from the hostel and various friends from the sports club. Ellen was amazed that everyone fitted in. Dirk took the ring from his inside jacket pocket and as he handed it to Daniel it slipped through his fingers and rolled away around the feet of the registrar. Dan chased it across the floor until he managed to grab it and put it safely in his pocket whilst Ellen looked on in horror. First he was late for her wedding and then he dropped the ring. She was beginning to wonder what else could blight her wedding day. She hoped it wasn't an omen.

The day had been a complete fiasco, but when it was all over and they were back in their room at the Kawena Hills, which Dan had reserved for their first night of married life, they rolled on the bed laughing at the absurdity of it all.

'You may well laugh,' said Ellen trying hard to stay serious with tears running down her cheeks. 'I very nearly didn't marry you. I thought you'd run away. If you hadn't turned up when you did I was going to tell Ben to take me back to the hostel. And as for dropping the ring……. ' she shook her head, 'there's no hope for us.'

'Ah, but you love me, Mrs Du Plessis,' teased Daniel, tickling her and smothering her with kisses.

'I suppose I do,' laughed Ellen. 'I must be out of my mind.'

# Chapter 10

THE NEXT DAY they drove three hundred miles down to Salisbury, the capital of Rhodesia. Mick had secretly tied tin cans onto the back of the jeep and put a sign on the back saying 'Beware, Honeymooners'. They made a terrible racket until they were well out of Lusaka and then they stopped at the side of the road by an African village and untied them watched by a group of giggling potbellied children. As they drove Ellen rested her hand on Daniel's knee and serenaded her new husband with songs from South Pacific.

Showing her passport at immigration control Ellen suddenly realised she was still Ellen Sanderson. That was something she would need to change when they returned to Lusaka. She would have to change her name on all her documentation; her passport, driving licence and identity card to Ellen du Plessis. She smiled. She liked the sound of that. It rolled off the tongue, Ellen du Plessis.

It was late-afternoon when they drove into the city. The wide clean avenues bordered by tall white buildings made Ellen feel as if the ocean was at the end of every street. They were booked in at the Routledge Hotel which was part of the Kawena Group where the Manager had arranged for them to have the honeymoon suite.

The suite was luxurious with thick white carpets and a deep sprung king sized bed. An enormous arrangement of white roses and lilies stood on the corner of the dressing table to welcome them, and outside the window there was a balcony where you could step out and look over Jameson Avenue to Central Park. After dinner they took a glass of wine out there and watched the huge blood-red sun setting over the trees leaving the sky flushed with a deep rosy glow.

'Here's to us,' said Daniel, lifting his glass, his eyes sparkling.

'To us,' Ellen had never been so happy. This was the start of a wonderful new chapter in their lives.

There was a knock on the door and Daniel jumped to open it. An Indian waiter in a smart royal blue uniform with a Routledge Hotel badge on the breast pocket, stood with a tray holding champagne in a bucket of ice and two champagne flutes.

'Compliments of the Manager,' he said, bringing it in and placing it on the bedside table. 'Please let reception know if there's anything else you require, Sir.' He bowed and left.

When he'd gone Daniel smiled at his wife and took her in his arms, 'I have everything I need right here,' he murmured as he kissed her hair? She felt his hands pulling down the zip of her dress and unfastening her bra. She shook her hips and hunched her shoulders as they fell to the floor leaving her in just her panties. Then she helped him off with his shirt and undid his shorts. They quickly rid themselves of their underwear, their naked bodies eager to find each other, caressing and kissing until caressing and kissing were no longer enough. Daniel lifted Ellen and laid her gently on the bed. He peppered kisses on to her tummy adoring the smoothness of her body so much softer than his own. He loved the feel of her, the curve of her hip and the softness of her breast. She was everything he'd ever dreamed of, soft and warm and lovely. As his kisses became more demanding he felt the need to possess her completely, be part of her. She gasped as she felt the hardness of his body against her own. The waves of their passion grew to a crescendo of ecstasy before abating leaving them both weak and satisfied.

They lay back exhausted on the magnificent king-size bed their legs entwined.

'Wow!' gasped Ellen as she kissed Daniel's shoulder. She smiled dreamily 'that was incredible.'

Daniel sat up and reached for the champagne. 'Time for a celebration.' He poured two glasses and gave one to Ellen. 'Here's to us and great sex.' His brown eyes twinkled wickedly.

'I'll second that.' She sipped and made a face as the bubbles fizzed up her nose, her limbs turning soft and runny like melting chocolate as the wine warmed and excited her. Daniel smiled lazily tracing his finger from her cheek, down the side of her neck and onto her breast.

'I think…' he laughed and took her glass, '…you've had enough of that for now.'

'What? Again? So soon? You're insatiable,' she chuckled.

She felt his chest brush her breast as he leaned over her and put her glass on the bedside table then kissed her gently letting his fingers trail down over her hardening nipples. 'Only with you, my gorgeous girl,' he laughed whilst his hands caressed her body once again.

They slept content in one another's arms that night certain that life would be perfect from now on as long as they had one another.

# Chapter 11

ELLEN LOVED SALISBURY with its wide avenues skirted by purple blossomed jacaranda trees. She couldn't wait to mooch around the big department stores and buy some fashionable new clothes, so on the second afternoon she left Daniel meeting up with some colleagues in the Routledge bar whilst she enjoyed herself wandering around the two big department stores. There was a sale on in Barbour's so she bought a pair of jet elephant ear rings for Joanne and a soft leather purse for Sally. Then she crossed the road and went through the revolving glass doors of Sanders and took the lift to the dress department on the second floor. She'd not seen such fashionable clothes since she'd left England and she bided her time admiring the dresses on the rails until she came upon a lovely sapphire blue strapless number. She carried it into the changing room and tried it on then came out and looked at herself critically in the mirror. It was gorgeous. Dan would love it. 'That really suits you, Madam,' said a saleswoman behind her. 'It brings out the colour of your eyes and it's real silk. How about some shoes to go with it?' She showed Ellen a pair of silver sandals with three inch heels. Ellen looked at them longingly. She already had some sandals but these were so sexy.

'What the hell?' thought Ellen after she'd tried them on. 'I'll take both.' It wasn't every day you got married. Having paid for her purchases she made her way to the lift and pressed the button for the top floor. The door slid open into the Birdcage Roof Restaurant, a popular meeting place where Salisbury housewives sat at tables surrounded by their shopping bags chatting to their friends over tea and cake. Exotic potted ferns and palms were dotted around, and here and there a canary twittered in a gilt cage. Over the balcony she could see the tops of Salisbury's tall white buildings and in the distance she could just spot a kopje with a wireless mast on top. She sat down at an empty table and ordered a pot of Lady Grey and a toasted tea cake. As she poured tea from a floral teapot into a matching china cup she admired the svelte models in their chic ensembles, gliding between the tables showing off the latest wedding guest outfits. Big wide brimmed hats appeared to be in fashion with simply cut straight calf length dresses, matching jackets and very high heels. She couldn't quite see her friends in Lusaka wearing them but they weren't out of place in Salisbury. It was all so sophisticated; a complete contrast to OK Bazaars and the dusty avenues of Lusaka.

It was a beautiful barmy summer afternoon so she strolled into Cecil Square and sat with her bags on a bench overlooking vibrant flower beds of bright red cannas.

An African woman in a colourful scarf tied turban style behind her head, wandered by and, seeing a prospective customer she laid out her crochet work on a blanket in front of Ellen.

'Look mama, I give you good price,' she said holding up an intricate table cloth which must have taken weeks of work and would have cost a fortune in Barbour's. Ellen smiled and shook her head,

'How much for these dolls?' she asked picking up two crocheted dolls with wide red woollen smiles. The price was too high but haggling was expected. After bargaining good naturedly for a few minutes she bought one for each of Sally's little girls and the woman was satisfied. Now she had to find something for the boys. As she left the park she passed a crippled man on the pavement selling wire animals on long wire handles which galloped along on rickety wheels when you pushed them. He sat on the ground with his back up against the fence wearing a shirt and trousers which had seen better days and had probably been thrown out by a European housewife getting rid of her husband's old clothes. He looked at her with one milky eye and grinned a toothless smile. 'You buy Madam. I give you good price.' That seemed to be a popular turn of phrase amongst the street vendors.

'Did you make these yourself?' she asked pointing to one. He nodded, struggled to his feet and demonstrated how the toy worked.

'O.K.' said Ellen. 'I'll take two.' She liked to support the African handicrafts. They had so little yet they used their skills to make their creative wares out of nothing. She hoped one day the time would come when they would have the education they needed to use their inventiveness in other ways. It always seemed a pity to Ellen that the country was missing out on such a rich resource of ingenuity.

When she arrived back at the hotel she went up to the room and left her parcels on the bed, then made her way down to join Daniel in the bar.

'Ah there you are,' said Dan, standing up to kiss her on the cheek. 'I thought you'd left me. Come and meet Maurice. He's the manager here. Maurice this is my wife Ellen'.

Maurice stood up and offered his hand. He was tall and tanned like most Rhodesians with a receding hairline and twinkling blue eyes.

'So how do you like Salisbury Mrs du Plessis?'

It was the first time anyone apart from Daniel had called her that and it sounded strange to Ellen.

'It's beautiful, Maurice, and please call me Ellen. I've just been sitting in Cecil Square. It's a peaceful spot right in the middle of the city.'

'We have a lot of beautiful places for you to visit, Ellen,' said Maurice obviously proud of his city. 'You must take your wife into Central Park, Dan. And take her up the kopje as well. You can see the whole of Salisbury from there. Now if you'll excuse me I have work to do. Enjoy your evening.'

He left them and as he went Ellen noticed he had a slight limp. Daniel told her it was as a result of a riding accident when he was a boy.

'He was a keen rugby player when we were at school,' said Dan. 'He had aspirations to play for Rhodesia, but one day a leopard got into the paddock on his father's farm whilst he was exercising his horse and the horse bolted. Maurice was thrown over a fence and his foot got caught in the stirrup. The horse landed on top of him then got up and carried on running dragging old Maurice behind him. Maurice was lucky to survive. Poor guy was in hospital for months. They saved his leg but it put paid to his rugby career.'

Ellen wondered if everyone had been at the same school in Rhodesia. It seemed a very close knit community. 'What happened to the leopard?' she asked.

Daniel shrugged, 'It disappeared. Now tell me, you've been out ages. What've you been spending all your money on?'

'I've bought some prezzies for Joanne, Sal and the kids, and something really nice to wear but you won't see it till you take me out on the town. It's a surprise.'

'How about me?' teased Daniel, 'did you by any chance buy me that Mercedes sports I told you about?'

'You don't need a Mercedes sports. You've got me,' she replied with a pretend pout.

He laughed, 'OK, how about I take you out tomorrow night. Tonight I thought we'd have an early dinner here and then have an early night,' he grinned mischievously and Ellen blushed. She would have liked to go up the kopje but they could do that another time. An early night with her new husband was a more exciting prospect. There was an hour until dinner so he picked up their drinks and they went to sit in the lounge where a Sinatra lookalike was tinkling out old favourites on an ivory grand piano entertaining the hotel guests with requests.   Daniel went across and whispered something in his ear.

A second later he began to play *Strangers in the Night*.

# Chapter 12

THE FOLLOWING DAY Daniel said he had to meet up with some business contacts, he seemed to know so many people in this city, so Ellen was happy to stay around the hotel for the afternoon and enjoy the luxury of a massage and a manicure. Relaxing on her tummy soothed by soft music and the aroma of jasmine and vanilla oil, she planned what they would do that evening whilst the masseuse gently kneaded her shoulders. After this she would have her nails polished with the latest pretty pink shade, and then she would put on her new silk dress which she'd bought the day before at Sanders so that Daniel could take her out to that expensive Thai restaurant on Gordon Avenue. She'd heard they opened the doors onto the veranda in the evenings so you could dance outside in the moonlight. It seemed a perfect place to show off her new dress and spend a romantic evening.

Back in the room she slipped on the sapphire silk dress which made her eyes even bluer and admired herself in the wardrobe mirror. 'Not bad for a Manchester mouse,' she thought as she pirouetted on her silver heels. Then she wrote a quick note for Daniel and propped it up on the dressing table in case he wondered where she was. She closed the door and took the lift down to the busy sunken hotel lounge on the ground floor to spend an hour listening to 'Frank Sinatra' on the piano. As she walked in he looked up and smiled at her whilst beginning to play *Strangers in the Night*, the song Dan had requested for her the day before.

She sat close to the piano next to an archway which led out to the hotel entrance hall, watching for her husband to come in. She looked at her watch. His business meeting had obviously gone on longer than he expected, but she was sure he'd be back soon. She checked with reception to see if he'd left a phone message but he hadn't so at six o'clock she went back to the room and waited. By 7pm she was feeling hungry and ordered room service. They could eat first and then go dancing later.

The meal arrived but no Daniel. Rather than let it go cold she ate hers in front of the T.V. feeling an undercurrent of resentment, whilst covering Daniel's meal with the silver dome to keep it warm. It was unusual for him to be so late without good reason. He was always so attentive. It got to ten o'clock and he still hadn't appeared. Her anger gave way to worry. Something was wrong, she was sure of it. She imagined he'd been involved in an accident and was about to phone the hospital when she heard the sound of a key grating in the lock. It seemed an age before the door opened.

'Hey Ell. I'm back' He was unsteady and his eyes were unfocussed. 'What's fer supper Sweetie Pie?' Ellen was furious. He would never have done this to her before they were married.

'Dan. Where've you damn well been? I've been worried sick about you.' She cried angrily.

'Jus' been at th'Ambassador with Mike 'n Sandy celebrating.' He staggered to the bed, fell onto it, missed it and rolled onto the floor. If she hadn't been worrying about him for the past four hours Ellen would have been amused but the anger was bubbling up inside of her. How dare he leave her on her own all day and come back drunk as a mule as if nothing had happened– on their honeymoon too. This wasn't how marriage was supposed to be. And who were Mike and Sandy? They didn't sound like business colleagues to her.

'I'll give you celebrating,' she shouted angrily. She bent down and shook him, wanting some answers, but it was no use. He was dead to the world. She glared down at him, frustrated at not being able to get a response. In disgust she left him on the floor and went to sleep in the spare bedroom next door. Tossing and turning she thought about what Sally had said to her on timeless occasions. *Don't get involved Ell. He's a great guy but he drinks, he gambles. He's broken scores of hearts in this town.* Was this the true Daniel? The one everyone but she could see. But she loved him. He was kind and sensitive and funny, not to mention very attractive. And she was sure he loved her. Eventually her brain was exhausted thinking about it all and she fell asleep but not before she'd vowed to have it out with him the next morning.

During the night she was woken as Daniel crawled into bed beside her. He snuggled up to her and nuzzled the back of her neck but she pretended to be asleep. She was in no mood for his lovemaking.

The next day he acted as if nothing had happened and when she challenged him he brushed it off, his face a mask of innocence.

'I told you I was meeting up with some business colleagues. We just lost track of time. You enjoyed your day didn't you?'

'Yes I did, but it would have been nice to go out with my husband last night like he promised instead of sitting in watching the T.V on my own. I was looking forward to it.

Got myself all dolled up in my new dress.  And you never even phoned me,' she added peevishly.

His eyes went dark as they always did when he was angry but he'd never directed his anger at her before.  'I'm sorry,' he said shortly.  He refused to talk about it anymore and she was the one left feeling guilty for getting mad with him.  It was their first row and it had happened on their honeymoon. Ellen hoped it wasn't a bad omen.

For the rest of the time everything was as it should be on a honeymoon.  Daniel was as attentive and loving as ever. But there were still questions at the back of Ellen's mind and she found it frustrating that Daniel would not communicate with her about his behaviour the night before.

Nothing more was said about the incident so Ellen decided it was best forgotten.  After all, she reasoned, she had left him on his own for a whole afternoon whilst she went shopping so it was only fair that he should have some freedom too.  They weren't children.  And so began the denial and the excuses.

# Chapter 13

THEY'D PLANNED TO make their way back to Lusaka via Kariba for a couple of relaxing nights by the lake. As they climbed in the jeep Daniel said, 'I'd like you to meet Liz and Johnny, old friends of mine. They live just outside Salisbury and we can pop in as we pass. They're expecting us.'

They pulled into the driveway of an elegant low stuccoed Spanish style house overlooking lawns sweeping down to the road. A red Volkswagen beetle and a cream Opel Estate with a dog guard in the back were parked outside a double garage. The studded front door was arched and there was a small slated patio in front of it with two chairs and a wrought iron table to one side. A short woman in her mid-forties with an ample bosom, dark cropped hair and a beaming smile came bouncing out to meet them wearing white shorts and a bikini top. A liver and white spaniel chased at her heels. She reached up and threw her arms around Daniel whilst the dog looked on, her little cropped tail wagging vigorously.

'This is my friend Liz' laughed Daniel when he'd unravelled himself. 'I've known Liz forever. She used to pick me up from school when I was a kid'.

'Welcome Ellen, and congratulations!' Liz hugged Ellen warmly. 'We've heard so much about you.'

'What a beautiful home you have, Liz,' said Ellen looking around her and taking in the terracotta roof tiles and arched windows with their ornamental grills.

'Thank-you, it's all down to Johnny. He's a builder and we worked on the design together when we first got married. We'd love you to stay over for a night or two if you can.'

'Wish we could' said Daniel regretfully. 'We're booked in to stay at the Kariba Boatel for two nights and then we have to get back. There's a big do on at the hotel on Saturday. We're opening the new wing. All the bigwigs are attending and I have to be there to make sure it all goes off smoothly.'

'Never mind. Another time. Johnny's out in the garden by the pool, Dan. Go through and chat whilst I get to know Ellen and show her my puppies.'

Liz took Ellen through to a room off the hallway where there was a basket with two little liver and white spaniel pups sleeping in it. A door lead out onto a penned area.

'This is my puppy rearing room,' explained Liz. 'Did Dan tell you? I breed spaniels.'

'No he didn't. They must take a lot of work.'

'Oh they do. That's why I only allow Mischa to mate every two years. That's my dog. But she's getting on a bit now so this might be her last litter.'

'They're adorable, Liz,' Ellen picked one up and it snuggled into her. 'How old are they?'

'Ten weeks. I had six and have found homes for five of them. Now I need someone to take that one off my hands. I don't suppose you'd like him?' She looked at Ellen appealingly

'I'd love him but we have no veterinary papers. They'll never let us through the border with him.'

'Oh I'm sure we can think of something. But come and say hello to Johnny. He's dying to meet you.'

Ellen put the pup back in the basket and looked longingly at it as she went out of the room.

She followed Liz into a large lounge area with four brown leather armchairs and a four seater settee. The floor to ceiling concertina windows were pulled right back to display a wide patio area and a swimming pool covered by a safety net. Daniel and Johnny were sitting opposite one another in the armchairs deep in conversation. They looked up when the girls walked in and both rose from their chairs.

'You're about to meet my best girl,' said Daniel proudly putting his arm around his wife.

Liz pouted, 'I suppose that means I'm demoted,' she said jokingly.

'You're a very close second, Liz,' quipped Daniel with a grin.

They sat and chatted for a while. Johnny seemed happy to let Liz do all the talking, mostly about her puppies, and during a brief break in the conversation he managed to ask Ellen about her job in Lusaka and how she found living and working in Africa.

'I'm loving it,' she replied. 'I've signed a contract for three years. I wasn't sure to begin with if that was too long in the present political climate, but it's nothing like what they are saying in the papers back home. Anyway, now I have a husband there's no question of leaving here,' She smiled fondly at Dan. 'The children here are a breath of fresh air and I've never been in a more peaceful spot.'

'Yes, well all the troubles are out in the bush between here and the Zambian border of course,' said Johnny. 'Our boys are managing to keep Mugabe's and Nkomo's terrorist activity away from the city, but the farmers and the townships along the northern border are having a tough time.'

'How long do you think it will last?' asked Dan. 'These sanctions must play havoc with the economy.'

Johnny puffed on his pipe thoughtfully, 'Hard to say, Dan. Depends on how long Ian Smith can hold out against the British Government. He's a pretty stubborn fellow is our Ian, ex war hero and all that, and the white population are behind him all the way, and some of the blacks too. They don't all follow those two thugs Mugabe and Nkomo. Smith won't give way to majority rule without a fight and so far we're managing to overcome any sanctions thrown at us. But these African leaders are pretty determined buggers too. What's more their boys are being trained in Russia. I think it'll get worse before it gets better.'

'I'm hungry' chipped in Liz, obviously bored with the political conversation. 'Let's have some lunch.' She got up and made her way to the kitchen where her maid Bella was busy preparing a salad. 'Ellen leave the men with their politics and come and meet Bella,' she called. 'Bella's one of the family. She's been with us for twenty years. Bella this is Ellen all the way from UK.'

Bella giggled happily. 'Hello Ellen' she pronounced the name with an emphasis on the first syllable. 'How are you?' she said in her melodious sing song voice, holding out her hand. 'Welcome to Rhodesia.'

'Bella's my best friend,' said Liz. 'She knows everything about me and I know everything about her.' Bella laughed and carried on placing cold chicken on a platter.

Lunch was a casual affair with the cold chicken and salads served on a lazy Susie in the centre of the table. Liz then produced a milk tart which she told them she'd made from a recipe handed down from her South African grandmother; a sort of egg custard but with an extra flavour Ellen couldn't quite put her finger on. Liz told her it was a drop of kirsch added to the filling. Delicious. Ellen had two helpings.

She was immediately drawn to Liz and Johnny. She felt comfortable with these warm friendly people who possessed an old world charm and obviously thought the world of Daniel. Johnny was some years older than Liz in his late fifties. He was a thickset man with a stoop which made him seem shorter than he was. Ellen liked his open face and ready smile. His laid back quiet nature contrasted well with that of his warm exuberant wife and they suited one another perfectly. Ellen could see that Daniel was relaxed in their company although she noticed no one mentioned Daniel's parents. One of these days she would ask Joanne about them but in the meantime it remained a closed subject. They chatted about old times and there was no 'putting on an act' as she sometimes thought he did with his friends in Lusaka. As much as Ellen loved Zambia with its raw beauty and exciting experiences she often felt that it was a very transitory place. There were too many contract workers from various parts of the world who were only there for a short while to make as much money as they could before moving on. It was a hail-fellow-well-met sort of place and not somewhere to make life-long relationships. Whereas here in Rhodesia people had been born here, grown up, got married and had families over four generations. This was their country. They'd built it up from raw bushland over hundreds of years and they weren't about to let it go.

Soon it was time to leave.

'Dan I've got something for you,' said Liz, her brown eyes sparkling mischievously. 'A small wedding present. Do you want to come through and I'll give it to you.' She led him out and Ellen was left with Johnny. He sat in his well-worn leather armchair in a pair of buff coloured shorts and an open neck shirt puffing on a pipe with Mischa sprawled across his feet. He smiled at Ellen paternally.

'It's been a pleasure meeting you, Ellen,' he said. 'Dan needs someone like you to keep him grounded and I can see how much you mean to one another. But take my advice and don't let him wind you around his little finger. He's a great guy but he needs a firm hand does our Dan.' He tapped the bowl of his pipe into a deep ceramic dish on the table next to his chair and the ashes fell out. Then he stood up and held out his hand.

'Don't leave it too long before you come and see us again,' he said sincerely.

Ellen took his hand, 'thank-you, Johnny. We will. I feel as if I've known you both for years.' She reached up and pecked his cheek.

There was a shout from the hallway, 'Come on Sweetie, Time to go.'

'They walked out to the driveway where Daniel was already in the jeep. She climbed in and a bundle of fur jumped onto her lap licking her face.'

'What's this?' she asked in surprise.

'That's our wedding present to you,' laughed Liz. 'I've spoken to Dan and he agrees it will be fine. Here's a little sleeping pill, Ellen. It's quite safe. The vet gave it to me.' She handed Ellen a small white envelope 'Just give him half of it an hour before you go over the bridge and he'll go to sleep on the floor of the car for a couple of hours. No one will even know you've got him. He's had all his injections so he's good to go.'

Ellen wasn't so sure but if Daniel said it was OK it must be. Things seemed to be done with much less regard for rules and regulations in this part of the world. She just hoped they wouldn't be caught out. It had been bad enough being arrested for spying last time they were at Kariba. Now they were going to become smugglers. What next? She was sure that one of these days they'd end up in gaol!

They drove away, their arms waving out of the windows in the warm afternoon air with Liz shouting after them. 'Come and visit soon,' and throwing kisses whilst Johnny just stood by puffing pensively at his newly lit pipe until they were out of sight.

# Chapter 14

KARIBA LAKE WAS peaceful with silver ripples stealing towards the shore breaking in a shimmer of fizzing foam on the pebbly beach. Ellen and Daniel, lay on sun loungers by the pool, sipping ice cold lagers in the hot sun, enjoying the last afternoon of their honeymoon at the Kariba Boatel. Across the lake Ellen could just see the rondavels at Siavonga where she'd spent her first weekend at the lake. Soon they would be making the two hour journey home across the border to Lusaka, and they wanted to make the most of the afternoon sun.

Daniel looked at his watch. 'It's four thirty now. We need to get away in half an hour if we want to make it through the border post by six.' He looked down at the liver and white spaniel puppy lying contentedly beside him.

'What time do you reckon we should give Bozo here his sleeping pill?'

Ellen reached over lazily and opened her purse which lay on the small table between them. She took a piece of folded toilet tissue from the small envelope and unwrapped it to reveal a tiny white tablet.

'Liz said to give him half of this about an hour before.' She used her finger nail to split the tablet in two.

Once again she wondered how they had come to be in this position.   Here they were, about to try and get a bouncing ten week old puppy from one country to another without veterinary papers.  It was crazy.  Why on earth had she allowed Liz to persuade them to do it?  But Liz had been insistent.

'Let's just hope this works,' sighed Ellen, opening the pup's mouth and closing it around the half tablet whilst stroking its throat to encourage it to swallow.  It rewarded her by jumping onto her lap and licking her face enthusiastically.

'There that should do it.  Now we must wait.'

And wait they did; watched and waited for the pup to fall asleep.  But he wanted to play.  No way was he going to sleep.  He pulled on his lead wanting to join some children running around the tables, jumped up and down and chased his tail getting himself all tangled up.  It got to 5 o'clock.

'Come on.  Let's go.  We'll not get home tonight if we miss the border.  It closes at six,' Daniel warned.

'But what shall we do with *him*?' Ellen despaired, pointing at the demented pup.

'We'll cross that bridge, literally, when we come to it. Come on. It's time to go.'

Daniel picked up their bags whilst Ellen undid the lead from around the table leg, and they made their way to the motel car park.

'Do you think I should give him the other half of the sleeping tablet?' asked Ellen doubtfully.

'Better not, just in case. We don't want to put him to sleep permanently,' said Daniel with a weak attempt at humour. 'It'll be fine. Stop worrying.'

When they arrived at the Rhodesian border post on the near side of the bridge, they parked the car as far from the building as they could and left the pup on the back seat. It seemed to be fairly quiet. Maybe it was asleep! They filled in forms and then approached the counter where a European Customs Officer in a crisp white uniform asked them 'Have you anything to declare, Sir?'

Daniel was just about to tell a big lie when the officer lifted his arm and pointed to the car park behind him. 'Is that your car, Sir?'

Ellen's heart did cartwheels and landed up in her stomach.

'What? Oh er, yes.' It was pointless for him to deny it seeing as theirs was one of only two cars there.

'Have you got papers for that animal, Sir?' asked the officer suspiciously.

Daniel turned around to see Bozo with his paws on the dashboard, his brown face looking out through the windscreen.

'Er no.' Daniel decided to plead ignorance. 'What sort of papers?'

'You need veterinary clearance papers to take an animal across the border, Sir. I can let you take it out but I have to warn you that if the Zambians won't allow the dog in without papers, I cannot allow it back into Rhodesia again.' Obviously in Rhodesia there was more respect for the law than on the Zambian side.

Daniel didn't know what to do. He had to be back at the hotel tomorrow. All the bigwigs would be there. No-one else could deal with such an important event. He stood and thought of the worst scenario, he and Ellen stuck on the middle of the bridge in No man's land clutching the lead of a highly active spaniel pup. He pushed the thought from his mind.

'OK,' he said with a resigned sigh. 'We'll have to risk it'

Ellen wasn't so sure but what could they do? It was too late to go back and this event at the hotel meant too much to Daniel. It very probably meant a promotion and a huge increase in salary if it went well.

Stamp! Stamp! 'Next one please.'

Back in the car neither spoke as they drove the short distance across the dam wall which divided Rhodesia from Zambia. When they reached the other side there were queues of people waiting to be dealt with and the car park was full, except for one space close to the small thatched building.

'It looks like we can't park as far away as I'd hoped,' groaned Daniel. 'We'll just have to take our chances and hope they're too busy to notice.'

They joined the queue of subdued home bound holidaymakers. Ellen hoped fervently that the busy African customs officers wouldn't notice their illegal contraband. It was already five minutes to six and hopefully they would be wanting to get home.

Suddenly the blare of a car horn shattered the quiet of the evening. Everyone turned around to see what was going on.

Oh no! There, as large as life, was Bozo, his tongue hanging out and a big grin on his face, with his front paws planted firmly on the horn, determined not to be ignored.

*That's it* thought Ellen as her pen hovered over the questions on the customs form. 'Have you any livestock?' Tick. No point in denying it now. She gave the form to the black officer and held her breath waiting for the inevitable questions and rejection.

Stamp! Stamp! She couldn't believe it. He'd not questioned it! They were free to go. They hurried out of the border post before he changed his mind. Bozo of course was now fast asleep on the back seat!

A hundred yards from the border post the wide sand road swept around a bend. Daniel stopped the car.

'What are you doing?' asked Ellen nervously.

Daniel didn't say a word. He just opened the car door and walked shakily around to the boot.

He got back into the car holding a bottle of vodka. 'I need a drink!' he said, unscrewing the cap. He then drank half the bottle before turning the key in the ignition and began driving back to Lusaka up the twisting road of the escarpment

# Chapter 15

BY THE END of the year Daniel had become General Manager for the Kawena Group in Zambia which meant he had more responsibility, more travelling and more entertaining to do, and of course, there were lots of parties and plenty of alcohol. They attended hotel functions about once a month which at first were fun. Daniel was his usual amusing self and everyone loved him. He was witty and entertaining and she was proud of her handsome clever husband when she saw the envy in other women's eyes. She saw a lot of Joanne who also attended most of the hotel functions and they were becoming good friends.

One day they met for lunch by the lily pond where Ellen had first met Daniel. It was a Monday and fairly quiet.

'This place holds so many happy memories for Daniel and me,' said Ellen. 'I'm so sad that your mom and dad couldn't share our big day. What were they like Jo?'

Joanne was silent for a few moments staring into the pool lost in thought and Ellen was worried that she'd pushed her too hard.

'They were beautiful; the perfect couple. We had a wonderful childhood, Ellen. We had a caravan, only a little 4 berth, and we used to go for holidays out into the bush and watch the animals and the birds, just the four of us. I have a photo of them in my purse. Would you like to see?' She fished in her purse and brought out an old black and white photograph of a tall handsome man, not unlike Daniel, with his arm around a willowy long legged blond with fine features. They were standing in front of a small four berthed caravan. Ellen could see where Daniel and Joanne had got their good looks. 'Dad knew so much about wild life,' continued Joanne. 'We would take binoculars and pass them around whilst he told us the names and habits of the birds and animals. Things were so peaceful in those days. None of the nonsense we get now. Then dad bought a little putt putt boat and we'd go out on the river and catch tiger fish. Dad would gut it and Mom would spice it and wrap it in foil for dad to cook over the camp fire. It was delicious.'

She stopped with a faraway look on her beautiful face. Ellen kept quiet. She wanted to hear more. She wanted to know about the accident.

'And then suddenly they weren't there anymore,' continued Joanne quietly, a tear glistening in the corner of her eye.

'What happened,' urged Ellen gently.

'Oh it was one of those stupid accidents. We'd been out to the Falls. We'd had a lovely day walking through the rain forest and mooching around the African market buying curios. Dan was driving. He was twenty-one, just got his first car, a blue ford corsair. He was really proud of it. And I was nearly eighteen. Josh and I were going to be married in two months' time. We'd been childhood sweethearts since we were fourteen. Were in the same class at school. Anyway Dan had had a couple of beers in the bar of the Vic Falls Hotel, not a lot. Dad didn't know or he wouldn't have let him drive. Anyway Dad was in the passenger seat. Mom, Josh and me were squeezed in the back. We were driving along this straight narrow strip road when without warning a kudu came leaping out of the bush right in front of us. Daniel swerved to miss it and the next thing we were out of control ploughing through the bush heading for this baobab tree. I can't remember anything after that. When I came to...' She stopped and sobbed, 'mom was lying back next to me. She wasn't breathing. I did my best to revive her but it was no good. I think her neck was broken.' She sobbed, 'she'd gone. Dad had gone through the windscreen. It was awful Ellen. All I can remember is blood everywhere. Daniel had been thrown out and ended up with nothing more than a broken arm and a few scratches.  I was treated for concussion.  We were the lucky ones.'

Ellen put her hand out and stroked Joanne's shoulder sympathetically 'I'm so sorry, Jo.  What about Josh?  Did he survive?'

'Yes, but he lost a leg and his face was all smashed up. Somehow things weren't the same for us after that.  Not for me but for him.  I'd have looked after him if he'd let me, I loved him, but he was proud.  He cancelled the wedding plans and took himself off to God knows where and I haven't seen him since.'    Joanne's story put Ellen's experience with Eric in perspective.  They sat in empathetic silence for a few minutes.  Ellen didn't know what to say to comfort her sister in law so she kept quiet.

'It affected Dan very badly.  He blamed himself.  That's why he drinks and gambles so heavily, to blot out the guilt.' She smiled at Ellen, 'But now you're in his life it'll get better. I know it will.'

Ellen hoped she was right.  At least now she knew what drove her husband.  Maybe if she was able to talk to him about the accident it would be out in the open.  Isn't that what psychotherapists did?

# Chapter 16

THEY'D BEEN MARRIED a year and having Ellen in his life didn't seem to be making things any better. He wouldn't talk about his mother and father or the accident and he seemed irritated that she knew about it. If anything the drinking had gotten worse. It didn't matter whether the occasion was happy or sad, it would be an excuse to get drunk. He didn't seem able to have just one or two drinks like anybody else. Once he started he had to get paralytic. But it wasn't only Dan who was changing, she was too. It was becoming an obsession to mark the bottles in the booze cabinet, and she got that she was constantly sniffing his breath when he came in the door. Whilst his behaviour became more and more erratic, she felt powerless to do anything about it. If she mentioned it there would be a huge row and he wouldn't speak to her for days, so she kept quiet hoping the problem would go away.

She didn't realise the silent treatment was mental abuse until she found she'd stopped speaking her mind altogether, she was so scared of the consequences. If only he would communicate with her she was sure they could sort this problem out. But he wouldn't or couldn't. She began to think she was in a one sided relationship which she couldn't walk away from.

She'd stopped bothering to cook a proper meal in the evening as Dan was rarely there for the food she prepared. He reckoned he could grab a meal at the hotel to save her the trouble before going down to meet up with their friends at the club. It was all about getting in as much drinking time as possible and hiding it from her. It seemed to Ellen that now they were married, she ceased to be a novelty, he didn't have to pay attention to her needs anymore. It was no wonder his first two marriages had failed if this was the way he'd behaved. But Sal had warned her so she only had herself to blame. Without her husband's attention she was lonely. She comfort ate on cakes and chocolate to make her feel better, with the result that she'd gone up two sizes and was told unceasingly that she was getting fat and unattractive. Daniel seemed intent on making her feel bad about herself these days. She couldn't understand the change in him. What had she done to make him treat her so badly? Was it a reflection on how bad he felt about himself?

The Annual Directors' Dinner at the Kawena Hills was due to take place in three months. It was a formal occasion with full evening dress. Ellen had bought a beautiful slinky black figure hugging number on one of their trips down to Salisbury before she put on weight, and she hadn't had a chance to wear it yet, so she set herself a goal to get back to her normal weight. She went on a strict diet and exercised rigidly every morning and evening, running on the spot, sit ups and hip rolls, and now when she looked in the mirror she was a svelte size ten, something she had never been before. On the night of the Dinner she dressed carefully, pinned a pair of dangly jet ear rings in her ears which Dan had bought for her when they first got married, and looked at herself critically in the mirror. She looked fantastic. Daniel was looking as slim and handsome as ever in a dress suit with a midnight blue cummerbund, sparkling white shirt and bow tie. Together they looked like the golden couple. Daniel whistled his approval as she presented herself to him and she felt really good about herself. At last she had a positive reaction from him. She was happy.

The evening went well and the wine flowed freely. Dan had just made a speech which was slightly slurred but he still managed to make his audience laugh. Unsteadily he sat down and missed the chair ending in an undignified heap on the floor.  She rushed to help him but he waved her off angrily,

'I'm fine.  Leave me alone,' he growled, his eyes darkening as he struggled to his feet.

Ellen saw the looks of disdain in people's eyes.  She was ashamed to watch him making a fool of himself when he'd always attracted looks of admiration.  Drinking was a popular pastime in Lusaka but anyone who couldn't hold their liquor was the subject of hypocritical jibes and became a social pariah.

That was when people stopped inviting them to their homes for weekend barbecues and very soon Ellen felt isolated.

One night when she and Joanne were sitting in the busy club bar watching a poker game at which Daniel was losing heavily she sought some support from her sister-in-law

'I'm worried about Daniel,' she said, 'He's drinking far too much and losing a lot of money in these poker games.  I don't know what to do about it, Jo.'

Joanne shrugged, 'You're the only one with a problem as far as I can see, Ellen,' she said refusing to accept that it was her brother with the problem.  'You need to relax and cut him some slack.  You're so tense these days.  No wonder he'd rather be here than at home.'  Ellen was shocked at her tone. She'd expected more sympathy from her friend, but Joanne absolutely idolised her brother. As far as she was concerned he drank because he wanted to blot out the past and he played cards to relax. She would make any excuse rather than face up to the truth. Then she'd made an excuse to go and talk to friends on the other side of the room and walked away. Ellen felt rejected but she didn't want to lose their friendship so she kept her thoughts to herself. Thankfully she still had Sally who never failed to sympathise with her, but Sally couldn't understand why she stuck around. Neither did she if the truth were known, but she did. She wasn't even sure if she loved him anymore but she was too proud to admit she was beaten, especially to Sally who had advised her not to marry Daniel in the first place. With no one who understood she became more and more isolated and depressed. It seemed she was the only one in the world with a husband who was drinking himself into oblivion.

# Chapter 17

DANIEL BEGAN STAYING out later and later at the club and many evenings Ellen would sit alone, just watching the window for his car lights to appear.   There would occasionally be a knock on the door late at night and a friend would be standing there telling her that Dan was involved in a poker game and needed his cheque book.  He seemed to resent her going down to the sports club these days, telling her she was spying on him which made Ellen think that maybe he'd found someone else, someone more appealing. After all he had a track record.  Maybe he was with her now. She imagined him flirting with one of the many unattached women who hung around the bars he frequented.  He was such an attractive man she was sure she would lose him.  All her old insecurities came back to torment her.  First Eric, now Daniel.  What was wrong with her?  She didn't want to be jealous and possessive, but she found herself one day searching his pockets to see if there was any evidence of his betrayal.  All she found was a business card with a note scribbled on the back: *Ellen, Dan never stops talking about you.*

*You can't be so bloody perfect.* Ellen felt embarrassed. She felt as if she'd been caught in the act; it wasn't like her to behave so badly. What was happening to her? And why couldn't he say these things to her instead of some loose woman sitting in a bar. He obviously still loved her. There must be something she could do to get their relationship back on track. Everyone kept telling her she should do something about it so she kept trying. She bought alcohol with her weekly shop and tried to encourage him to drink at home instead but it didn't work. She tried tempting him home with new recipes which she cut out from magazines, but she ended up eating for both of them and was rapidly putting on weight again. She spent her money on bits and pieces to titivate their home but he disregarded any attempts to make their home more attractive. She kept telling him she loved him to no avail. Nothing she said or did made any difference. The slippers by the fire routine just wasn't working.

In anger one night she poured the drink down the sink when she found a bottle hidden at the back of the wardrobe. When he came in he went straight through to the bedroom and she could hear him opening and closing cupboard doors. She held her breath and waited. There was a deathly hush. Then he came charging through and grabbed her arm.

'Where is it? What have you done with it?' he shouted angrily pinning her up against the wall until she sobbed. His face was ugly with anger and his eyes were dark and dead. She was terrified. Then he turned and left the house slamming the front door behind him. Ellen was sure the whole neighbourhood had heard him and was ashamed to look her neighbours in the face the next day.

Vehement arguments over his drinking became the norm but he wouldn't admit his problem and hit back at her by criticising her every move, sometimes in public. Ellen was deeply hurt. She couldn't believe that this was the charming man she'd married. One minute he was telling her she was unattractive and the next he was accusing her of having affairs. There was no rhyme or reason to it. It was as if his personality was gradually disintegrating from the cheerful optimistic man she had fallen in love with to a sarcastic abusive Mr Hyde who was constantly picking fights and finding fault. Whatever she did it always ended up being her fault. Nothing was ever Daniel's fault. Their marriage was being destroyed and she couldn't understand why this intelligent man was prepared to throw everything away when he could just stop drinking so much and everything would be back to normal again

Eventually his job was in jeopardy. She aided and abetted his lies by phoning the hotel on Monday mornings when he was suffering from a weekend hangover telling his secretary he had the flu or some other story she had concocted. But they all knew. It was as plain as a pikestaff. Why was she protecting him like this?

She lost all sense of what was true and false whilst her self-confidence gradually ebbed away along with her cheerful nature, which saw nothing to look forward to anymore. She felt as if she was being dragged under, with no life jacket to save her.

# Chapter 18

DANIEL SAT HUNCHED over the bar at the new airport which had been built recently out of town. He'd left the hotel in the good hands of Dieter, the Assistant Manager, and told him he had an important meeting to attend that afternoon with Customs and Excise. He wanted to see if he could cut the duty on a large import of towels and bed linen for the hotel. It might mean a backhander but he knew the customs officers down at the airport and was sure he could swing it. He'd done it before. Lusaka was that sort of place. A bribe in the right direction could work wonders.

The meeting had gone well and he now felt he needed to reward himself with a toddy or two. As long as Ellen didn't know about it he could get away with it and she couldn't nag him to death. She'd become a shrew of late, cross examining him whenever he came home. It was no wonder he stayed late at the club most nights. Who would want to go home to a nagging, suspicious wife? Couldn't a bloke have a bit of relaxation after a hard day's work without his wife constantly checking up on him? He ordered another double vodka and settled down to a couple of hours serious drinking, flirting outrageously with the young barmaid.

Finally he stumbled out of the bar, found his jeep, and fumbled the car keys into the ignition, eventually shooting out of the car park at a breakneck speed. The vehicle wove treacherously down the long dark road to Lusaka, its headlights bouncing off trees and scrub, narrowly missing a truck coming in the opposite direction. By the time he reached the town he desperately needed a pee so he stopped the car and prepared to relieve himself at the side of the road. If he was quick he'd just make the start of the poker game at the club.

An hour later back at the house Ellen was chewing the end of her red pen in the middle of marking her class's latest essays. The phone rang. She stretched out her hand and put the receiver to her ear. She wondered what the excuse would be this time. She'd got to the point where she didn't believe a word he said anymore.

'Sweetie I'm locked in my office. Immigration want my passport,' Ellen sighed heavily. He sounded the worse for wear as usual.

'Why do they want your passport, Dan?' she asked, beginning to feel like his mother. She had visions of their Kariba experiences catching up with them at last.

'Something to do with the company transferring money to Swiss Banks. I know nothing about it.'

'Shall I bring it round to you?' she asked, half believing him and eager to protect him as always.

'No, no. I'm not giving it to them. I'm holding out till they go away. Might never get it back. Jus' wanted you to know I've locked myself in and I'm sleeping here tonight.' He put the phone down before she could question him further and Ellen sat back wondering what was going on. It all sounded very far-fetched but as she'd discovered anything could happen in this country. It was difficult to know what was true or false these days. On the other hand he might be sleeping with someone else. She went to bed tormented by her imagination.

He arrived home the next morning looking as if he'd slept in his suit, hair awry, dishevelled but sober. Ellen looked at him critically and he avoided her eyes. Was this the man in the smart suit she'd married two years ago? She was tempted to question him but decided not to. He'd only get annoyed with her. And then he'd refuse to talk to her and she couldn't stand that. She wished they could have a shouting match. At least it would clear the air. But Daniel just sulked and avoided issues. As far as Ellen knew that was the end of the matter. Any suspicions she kept to herself, until a few days later when he came home with an official looking piece of paper headed *Notice of Prohibited Immigrant Status*. He slapped it down on the coffee table and walked off to pour himself a drink. Ellen picked it up and read it. They had four weeks to pack up and leave the country.

# Chapter 19

SHE DROVE OVER to see Sally and Ben the following evening to tell them the devastating news whilst Daniel was down at the club. They had no option but to go down to Rhodesia and beg accommodation with Liz and Johnny until they could sort themselves out. Daniel was sure he could get a transfer to the Routledge Hotel and Ellen could get a teaching job in the town. They were always short of qualified teachers in that part of the world. If only Daniel would curb his drinking habit everything would be alright. Maybe this was the lesson he needed.

Sipping a glass of wine with her friends in their peaceful lounge Ellen gazed out of the window at the gathering dusk whilst contemplating the events of the past few days. There was an aura of tranquillity as candlelight cast long flickering shadows on the walls. They had just eaten one of Enoch's delicious moussakas and the sounds of children's laughter echoed from the bathroom where Esta was bathing the children. Sally was wearing one of her homemade shifts and

Ben seemed to be wearing the same khaki shorts he'd been wearing on the day he met her at the airport. Sally had once told her that they were his favourites and she washed them when he went to bed and dried them overnight. They were such relaxing chilled out people with no airs and graces. Their place had become her haven where she was always assured of a sympathetic ear and a peaceful retreat. She'd miss them terribly.

Ben put his beer down on the side table and leant forward, 'do you know why Dan's been P.I.d?' he asked, taking a cigarette from a box of thirty Rothmans and lighting it up with a silver cigarette lighter.

'Well according to him it's because the Kawena Hills Group has been transferring funds illegally to Swiss banks.'

'That could be so,' replied Ben warily. Ellen looked at him sharply.

'Why? Have you heard something else?' She knew gossip was rife in the bars around Lusaka.

'I think you need to talk to Dan,' said Ben, jumping up and escaping into the kitchen to get another beer from the fridge.

Ellen looked at Sally, 'Well?' she asked pointedly, daring her friend to tell her the truth.

'Oh Ellen, you're my best friend. I did try to warn you but you were so in love with Daniel you couldn't hear me. Rumours around town are that Dan stopped his land-rover outside State House on his way home and began to urinate on the gates. He must have had a skinful somewhere and didn't know where he was. When a guard came to speak to him Dan took a swipe at him and ended up in a cell for the night.' Her lips twitched as she pictured the scene. 'It's funny really when you think about it but you can't go around disrespecting the Head of State. These guys get pretty sniffy about that. He's lucky he didn't get shot at!'

Ellen sighed wearily. It *was* funny, but it wasn't. No one in their right mind would put their future at risk by doing a daft thing like that. If it had been anyone else's husband she would have laughed, but it was *her* husband and she took it personally. Not only that, she was upset that he hadn't been honest with her. How could she trust him when he lied to her? She would have preferred to think of him in a prison cell for the night rather than in some other woman's bed. And now they had to get out of the country. Fortunately she still had her gratuity money in the bank which meant they would have a tidy sum to start off with in Rhodesia, which was just as well because Daniel didn't seem to have any spare money these days. Drinking and gambling were expensive hobbies.

'To be honest,' went on Sally, I think there's probably more to it than that. 'Word has it that Dan has been bribing customs officials. Someone's obviously spilled the beans. The authorities are just using this as an excuse to get him out of the country and out of their hair.'

Ellen shook her head. She was ignorant to all of this. Daniel's drinking was really out of hand. He'd never have taken such risks if he were sober. But the worst thing of all was that *she* was changing. She was no longer the happy go lucky girl who'd arrived in Lusaka three years before full of hope and excitement, and she didn't like the person she was becoming.

# Chapter 20

THEY SOLD THE few sticks of furniture they had, a bed and a couple of easy chairs, and they planned to buy more when they'd found somewhere to stay in Salisbury. Bozo was certified free of rabies by the vet and they were ready to go. He'd never lost the name Dan had given him at the Lake but it suited him so it stuck. Ellen wasn't sorry to leave Lusaka. Life there had turned sour for them. But she was sorry to say goodbye to Sally and Ben. They were the only real friends she had in that part of the world. Even Joanne had abandoned her after their little tiff in the club bar and they rarely talked intimately the way they used to do.

'Now you make sure you come and see us once we're settled,' she told Sally. For once Sally was silent as she hugged her friend tearfully. Ellen's heart was heavy. The smallholding and Sally's family had become an important escape for her during the past three years. She and Ben were such good friends, forever supportive. She was saddened that she would never enjoy the tranquillity of their home again.

They left two days later early in the morning, having said goodbye to all their friends at a farewell party at the club the night before, and headed for the border post at Chirundu. They were driving along quite fast and Ellen was beginning to let go of all the negatives from the past few months. The sun was shining, the sky was blue and they were off to start a new life, when suddenly grey shapes ambled out of the bush onto the road ahead, one very large and the other quite small. Daniel slowed and stopped some yards away and they watched as an elephant cow took her time crossing the road with her small calf which was barely out of the womb, following close on its mother's heels, its tiny trunk swinging from side to side and its squiggly little tail wagging happily. Ellen was mesmerised. Not to be left out Bozo sat up at the open window and barked. The female turned towards them and her ears began to flap, a sure sign of distress.

'Shut that bloody dog up for Christ sake, Ellen' shouted Daniel crossly as he began to back up away from the pair. Ellen turned around and put her hand on Bozo's collar. Daniel was getting more and more tetchy these days, but she let it go because he was probably stressed over the sudden move they'd had to make. She was getting like Joanne. Blaming anything but the booze.

'Sh! There's a good dog,' she stroked Bozo's neck. He stopped barking and whined softly. The elephant dropped its head towards its baby and its trunk curled protectively over its back. Happy that there was no longer a threat she then carried on into the bush. Daniel heaved a sigh of relief. 'Hell! That was close.' He took a half jack of vodka out of the glove compartment and took a swig.

'Steady on Dan.' said Ellen, more sharply than she'd intended. The events over the past month had made her anxious and irritable. 'We don't want to get to the border post with you stinking of booze.'

But he ignored her, his face taking on the brooding look she'd come to fear, and they continued their journey in heavy silence.

They crossed into Rhodesia and drove into the long Tsetse Fly control shed where border officials sprayed inside their car to kill any big brown Tsetse Flies that may have hitched a ride. Tsetse fly were the bane of the farmers' lives as they could infect the cattle with the dreaded sleeping sickness trypanosomiasis, humans too if they were unlucky. Then they headed, still without communication, towards Salisbury. Ellen hated these moods of Daniel's. Once he made up his mind not to speak to her it could last for days and no amount of wheedling on her part helped. He knew exactly how to upset her. She couldn't wait to get to Johnny and Liz's place where she knew the presence of his friends would break his silence. Just over an hour later they arrived at the charming Spanish house and were met by Liz and Johnny who were sitting on the front patio drinking coffee at a little wrought iron table waiting for their arrival.

'Welcome,' shouted Liz excitedly running over as the jeep drew up behind the VW. She hugged both of them warmly. 'Come inside, you must be tired. I'll show you to your room. You must stay here as long as you need.' She prattled on as she led Ellen inside

'Let me help you with your bags, Dan,' said Johnny tapping his pipe on the table and sliding it into the pocket of his shirt. 'Liz has been waiting for you for hours. I've had to give her a brandy to calm her down,' he shook his head and grinned at his wife's excitability.

Liz was delighted to be able to entertain her friends and Johnny quietly made them very welcome. Ellen suspected that Liz was a little bit in love with Daniel but she'd only ever experienced his charming side. However, as expected he changed from Mr Hyde into Dr Jekyll as soon as his friends came out to meet them and Ellen breathed a sigh of relief that his black mood was now dispelled.

# Chapter 21

THE FOLLOWING WEEK Daniel started work at the Routledge.  As an Assistant Manager it was a comedown from being Zambia's General Manager in Lusaka and his ego took a beating.  On one occasion in the first week Ellen had to phone Maurice to make excuses for him not being at work.  He'd stayed out late the night before and not arrived home till Johnny and Liz were in bed.  It wasn't a great way to start a new job.  One of the provisos that he was given the position was that he must curb his drinking habit.  One evening soon after they arrived Ellen managed to get Johnny to herself before Daniel came home from work.  They sat in the lovely big lounge overlooking the pool area whilst Liz was organising the evening meal in the kitchen with their loyal house servant Bella who'd worked for them ever since they were married twenty years before.

As always Johnny sat steadily puffing on his pipe and the sweet aroma of Virginia tobacco floated across to Ellen sitting in the other armchair.  She loved to sit quietly with

Johnny. He had such a calming influence on her and she needed all the calmness she could get at the moment. They sat in companionable silence for a while until Johnny said,

'Come on Ellen, out with it. What's wrong?'

She shrugged and shook her head, 'Daniel is going to lose this job if he doesn't watch out, Johnny. And we can't afford for him to be out of work.'

'Yes we have noticed he expects you to make excuses for him. You need to stop doing that you know Ellen. He's a big boy. Let him take responsibility for his own mistakes.' He puffed his pipe reflectively. 'Would it help if I talked to him?'

'Would you? He'll maybe listen to you.' They had dinner. Daniel wasn't home. He rushed in two hours later saying he'd had to work late. Ellen didn't say a word but Liz gave him a good maternal ticking off for not phoning and telling her whilst Johnny and Ellen gave each other knowing looks.

'Let's go out by the pool for smokes and coffee, Dan, and you can tell me how the job's going,' said Johnny, 'then Liz and Ellen can talk girl talk. Can you ask Bella to fetch our coffee outside please Liz?' They disappeared onto the patio and Johnny pulled the doors closed behind them.

Outside Johnny took the bull by the horns, 'Come on Dan. You're not being fair to yourself or to Ellen.' He picked up his pipe and began to press down some Virginia tobacco into the bowl and then lit it with a match from a box of Swan Vestas.

'What's she been saying?' asked Daniel visibly annoyed, puffing hard on his Rothman's.

'Only that she's worried about you. You can't afford to lose this job, Dan. But that's not all. That girl has stood by you through thick and thin and now it's your turn to stand by her. She's already been dragged down here and her life's been disrupted through no fault of her own. You need to pull it together, Dan, for the sake of your marriage.' There was no messing with Johnny. He told it as it was and Daniel didn't argue. Johnny was the only person he would take criticism from.

'I know, and I will. I know I can't afford to lose this opportunity, and I don't want to lose Ellen either.' He sounded really determined so Johnny left it at that. He was a man of few words but what he did say carried weight.

# Chapter 22

FOR THE NEXT few days Dan tried really hard. The need for liquor was strong but he avoided temptation by not going into the bar at lunchtime and by going home as soon as his shift was over. Ellen was hopeful that things were changing. It seemed as if they'd turned a corner and everything was going to be alright from now on. Without the liquor her husband became loving and caring once again. She'd always suspected that life in Lusaka wasn't good for him and she was sure that now they were away from the sports club things would be different.

She spent the weekend by the pool at Johnny and Liz's house scanning the ads in the Rhodesia Herald looking for a place to rent. She'd already been into the education offices and had begun teaching at Hatfield Primary School but it was a long way to drive over to Hatfield from Bluff Hill where Johnny and Liz stayed. It meant she had to rely on Daniel to drop her off in the jeep before going to the hotel. If they lived closer to her school she could get a lift with one of the other teachers until they could afford to buy her an old banger.

She enjoyed teaching at Hatfield. The children were well behaved and eager to learn and her colleagues were a friendly bunch who welcomed her to the team. She found teaching in Africa very different to England. Here they started lessons at eight o'clock and finished at one to avoid the heat. The afternoons were devoted to sport and clubs. Her afternoon activities were swimming and drama which she enjoyed doing. Every so often they had terrorist alert practises. If an attack was imminent there would be long blasts on an electric bell and the children had to dive under their desks and remain very quiet until the deputy head came to tell them all was well. Ellen wasn't sure just how effective that would be in case of a real attack but it gave the illusion of being prepared. One day they were all hiding quietly under their desks for half an hour waiting for the deputy who had forgotten to come around to her classroom on the far side of the school to give the all clear. In the end, when there was no apparent attack they crept out and resumed their lesson. It never ceased to amaze Ellen how much self-discipline the children seemed to have.

Meanwhile Daniel was settling into his position at the Routledge Hotel. After his chat with Johnny he'd cut his drinking right down and made up his mind to make a go of it. Organising the staff at the big hotel was taking up so much of his day that he had no time to think of spending time in the bar. Word was spreading amongst the local winers and diners that there was a new charismatic manager in charge of the restaurant and they flocked to eat there.

Everything seemed to be going well for a change and Ellen felt really hopeful.

One day, not long after they'd arrived in Salisbury, she was down at the school pool supervising a swimming lesson with the Year 4s when an older child ran into the pool enclosure with a note from the school secretary. Ellen read it and hurriedly spoke to her co-teacher.

'I have to go, Ian. There's been an emergency down at the hospital concerning Daniel. Can you cope on your own or shall I send a stand in?'

'You go Ellen. We're almost finished here. Don't worry, I'll be fine.'

# Chapter 23

SO NOW HERE she was, sitting on a bed in Ward 12 thinking back over their life together and hoping for some answers.

'Dan, what were you doing on that parapet?' She asked fearful of what the answer would be. He looked at her, his brown eyes once warm, now bleak and sad.

'They thought I was going to jump,' he said 'but I wasn't. I just needed a drink and I had to get out of there.' Ellen was relieved that at least it wasn't a suicide attempt.

'But why go out of the window, Dan? You must have known you were three floors up. Why not go out through the front door like everyone else?'

Daniel fidgeted nervously and plucked at the bed clothes. 'The sister was an old dragon and she was sitting on guard at a desk right outside my room. If it hadn't been for that damned buttress I'd have made it but I got stuck. It was bloody scary I can tell you,' he said with a hint of his old humour.

Ellen shook her head.  He must have been desperate to have done something so stupid.  This drink was destroying his power of reason as well as his body.  She hoped they would keep him in there for a while; at least whilst he was there she could relax and not worry about him.

'But why were you here in the first place?  You were fine when you dropped me off this morning.'

Daniel shook his head, 'I don't know what happened. One minute I was chatting to Maurice about staffing issues and the next I was in here.  I must have blacked out.'

A Doctor pushed back the curtain and came to speak to them.

'How are you feeling Mr du Plessis?'  Daniel mumbled that he felt fine, just a little shaky.

'I'm not surprised.  I'm going to prescribe something to calm you down; it'll help you with the seizure you had.  But you won't be able carry on this heavy drinking,' he warned sternly.

Daniel shook his head, 'I'm a social drinker, that's all,' denied Daniel stubbornly, 'nothing heavy.'

'You know Mr du Plessis we did an X-ray of your lower organs when you came in and they don't look very healthy. I have to tell you that if you carry on this "social drinking" of yours,' he made speech marks with his fingers, 'you will ruin your kidneys and your liver, you'll have more seizures and you'll be dead within a year.' He stopped to let Daniel absorb what he'd said. Daniel was silent.

'How long must he remain here?' asked Ellen, really worried now.

'I've advised that he stays here until he's been dried out. That'll take about three weeks. After that he's on his own.'

With that he left telling them he would leave a prescription with the Ward Sister.

# Chapter 24

DANIEL WAS DISCHARGED from Ward 12 three weeks later. When Ellen went to pick him up she found him cheerful and confident, ready to take on the world like the man she'd married. He was even organising the activities in the Ward so Ellen knew he was ready to come home. Within a couple of days he was back at work and enjoying the challenges which his new job presented. He was the old Daniel again, charming, energetic and irrepressible. What's more their lovemaking was more tender and passionate than ever. She dared to hope again.

Two months went by and he was still sober. By this time they'd rented a pretty little house near Ellen's school and they'd begun to talk about starting a family. Ellen felt confident that Daniel had learnt his lesson and she looked forward to the day when they could celebrate some good news for a change.

One evening she put on one of her prettiest dresses, sprayed herself with Je Revien and cooked a simple chicken dish. She laid the table carefully with some beautiful cut glass candle sticks Sally and Ben had given them as a wedding present, then she sat and waited for him to come home with the curtains of the patio window pulled back so that she could watch out for his lights. It was ten o'clock and dark when his headlights finally turned into the gateway. Her heart was a deadweight. She was sure that the nightmare had begun again.

'Sweetie, I'm sorry. We had an emergency at the hotel. There was a terrorist alert and we weren't allowed to leave.' She looked into his eyes and knew he was telling the truth. Believing he was lying was a habit she must break.

'What sort of terrorist alert?' she asked anxiously.

'Oh one of the customers spotted a suitcase which had been left unattended for a while in the hotel lobby. The whole place had to be evacuated until the bomb squad came and then it turned out it had been left there by someone who had gone out for dinner and just left it there to pick up later. But the silly bugger won't be doing that again. It had to be blown up.' Then he noticed the setting on the table and the new dress she was wearing, 'What's all this then?' he asked looking her up and down. 'You're looking very pretty tonight. What's the occasion?'

She raised her eyebrows and smiled impishly. 'We're pregnant,' she announced simply.

Daniel stood open mouthed then swooped her up in his arms. He was ecstatic. It was all he'd ever wanted. He was sure he was going to have a son.

# Chapter 25

NOT LONG AFTER she'd told him the good news they were sitting in the lounge debating what to have for supper when they heard car doors slam on the driveway. .

'Someone's here,' said Ellen, 'Have you invited anyone, Dan?'

'No.  It's probably Liz and Johnny,'

A familiar slim figure with long dark tresses passed the patio window.  It was over a year since they'd seen Dan's sister.

'This is a lovely surprise,' exclaimed Daniel.  'What brings you here little sis?  You should have told us you were coming.'

'I wanted it to be a surprise.  I have a friend with me. We're down here to buy an engagement ring,' she said with a sly grin.

'Well, let's meet him then.  Where is he?' asked Ellen

'I'm here,' said Dirk carrying in a heavy suitcase.

'Well I'll be...You sly old sod.' Dan clasped his friend's hand. 'When did this happen?'

'About a month ago,' said Joanne. 'Dirk invited me to go on the river in his new *Bezi Belle* and we just sort of found one another. Isn't that amazing after all this time?'

Ellen smiled. She wasn't surprised. 'That's fantastic news, Joanne, I always suspected you two would end up together. Have you made any plans for when? We'd love to be there but unfortunately Lusaka is out of the question for us as you know.' She hugged Joanne and whispered, 'I think Dirk found you years ago.' Joanne blushed. She had no idea the effect she had on men.

'We'd thought perhaps February next year. There's no rush' said Dirk, 'We want to be married here in Salisbury where all our old friends are. And I want you to be my best man.' He looked at Dan. It was the longest speech Ellen had ever heard him make. Obviously Joanne was good for him.

'That's wonderful. You must let us know how we can help with the arrangements,' said Ellen. She looked at Daniel and smiled, 'And now *we* have some good news for *you*. You're going to have a niece or nephew.'

'Make that a nephew' chipped in Dan.

Ellen laughed. 'Dan obviously knows something I don't.'

Joanne was thrilled.  She knew how much her brother had longed for a family.

'That's fantastic news, Ellen.  Congratulations both of you.  When is it due?'

'Around Christmas so make sure children are allowed at your wedding.'

'You bet.'

'Right this calls for a double celebration,' shouted Dan, in his element directing his troops.  'We'll go down to the Routledge for dinner on the house and take your Mercedes Dirk if that's O.K.  It's more comfortable.'

The girls sat in the back of Dirk's Mercedes whilst the boys caught up with Lusaka news in the front.

Joanne turned to Ellen, 'Ell, I heard about Dan's stay in hospital through the grapevine but I didn't get in touch because I was so ashamed of what I said to you that night at the club.  I was wrong but I couldn't see it.  Can you forgive me?'

Ellen put her arm through Joanne's and squeezed it. 'Nothing to forgive Jo.  Let's just begin again.  We both have so much to look forward now, and Daniel seems to be stable at last.  He doesn't drink at all these days.  I think the baby has made a difference.'

'Good.   Long may it last?'   That out of the way they settled down to discuss the forthcoming wedding and the latest gossip from the sports club.

# Chapter 26

ELLEN WAS THREE months pregnant and just beginning to show when Daniel came home one evening and said, 'How do you fancy some gentle game spotting Ell?' It had been a while since they'd been into the bush. It would do them both good to get back to nature again before the baby was born.

'I'm all for that,' agreed Ellen. 'But no river trips!'

Daniel smiled, 'No river trips.'

'Where do you want to go?'

Daniel grinned and tapped his nose, 'Just you wait and see. When's your next school hols?'

A month later during Ellen's mid-term break they packed the car and set off for a mysterious destination. She kept asking where they were going but he wouldn't tell her. It was a secret. All she knew was that they took the main road out of Salisbury towards Victoria Falls. As they neared the great waterfall they could hear the thunderous sound of water pounding down into the abyss and see the spray leaping hundreds of feet into the air. They pulled off the main highway onto a smaller untarred road and bumped over ridged sand for about 5 miles before turning up a sandy track at a rustic sign saying *Sundiata Lodge*.

'We're here,' shouted Dan as they drove into a circular driveway and stopped outside a low thatched building built of natural stone. Dan helped Ellen down from the jeep and they walked through a wide open entrance which led into a luxurious reception area with an open view through the other side looking out over the tops of trees in the Zambezi Valley. Zebra skins covered the rough white plastered walls whilst an expensive glitzy curio shop sat to the side displaying curios, jewellery, scarves and drums. Ellen eyed it all apprehensively and wondered where Daniel had found the money to pay for such an indulgence.

'Dan,' she whispered, 'are you sure we can afford all this?'

'Don't you worry, Sweetheart. It's all sorted,' he replied as he walked boldly up to the reception desk.

Ellen shook her head. What was he up to now?

'May I see Hennie please,' he asked the pretty receptionist who came to the counter.

'One moment please,' she disappeared through a door behind the desk and a few seconds later a tall sandy haired man in a safari suit appeared.

'Dan! Good to see you old friend. Glad you could make it.' He came from around the reception desk and they clasped hands. Dan turned to Ellen, 'Hennie meet my wife. Ellen, this is a very old friend of mine. He's the chief ranger here and he's invited us to stay as his guests for a few days.'

Ellen smiled, relieved. 'That's very generous of you, Hennie. Thank you. You have a beautiful place here.' Her husband was full of surprises. Hennie held out his hand to Ellen, 'You're welcome, Ellen,' and then noticing the obvious bump he winked at Daniel, 'I see congratulations are in order. We must celebrate later. Come. Let me show you to your cabin.'

Hennie led them up some wide rough steps carved into the rock and along a pathway to an elevated log cabin built onto the side of a rocky outcrop.

'This place only opened eighteen months ago,' he explained. 'The cabins are all built on different levels and surrounded by boulders so you will be very private. 'The owner is Alan Coetzee. You might remember him from school, Dan. He was a couple of years above us.'

'Ah yes, I remember him,' said Dan, 'I've played poker a few times with Al.'

'That's him. Anyway he won a lot of money on the roulette tables at Vic Falls and decided to invest in this place.

It needed some work doing to it so he bought it for a song and did it up. Then he found he needed someone who knew the bush to run the game park side. That's how I became involved. I met him in the pub one day and he offered me the job.' He unlocked the door of the cabin and gave Daniel the key, 'Right, let me show you around.'

They entered a lounge area with a slate floor and rough plastered walls bordered on one side by floor to ceiling sliding windows which ran the whole length of the cabin. There were three settees set in a square with a large heavy coffee table in the centre. A fridge was built into one wall. Ellen slid open one of the windows and stepped out onto a wide terrace bordered by a chunky wooden balustrade overlooking a large waterhole. In the distance zebra and wildebeest grazed peacefully together.

'There's booze in the fridge. Help yourself. It's on me,' said Hennie. Ellen held her breath.

'Not for me, nor Ellen' said Daniel. 'I'm a changed man. Going to be a dad.'

Hennie shot him a surprised look but didn't say anything. 'I'm going to leave you two to settle in now. We'll chat later.' He pointed to a cream telephone fixed on the wall, 'If you need anything just dial 9 and Jennie on reception will organise it. You may fancy going out for a drive in the park but make sure you're back by 6. We don't like people wandering around in there on their own after dark. Just give your cabin number to Wilson on the gate and he'll let you in.' With that he left them.

After he'd gone they investigated the rest of the cabin. An archway from the lounge led into a bedroom area with an enormous king sized four poster bed surrounded by mosquito nets tied back to the bed posts with cream satin ribbons. You could lie in bed and look out through the sliding glass doors at the waterhole fifty yards away.

'Wow!' said Ellen bouncing on the bed like a ten year old, her face beneath her blond curls a picture of pure delight, 'What luxury.' Daniel smiled as he watched her enjoyment. This is what he'd wanted. Just to see Ellen happy after all the trauma he'd put her through over the past two years. He had a lot of making up to do. It was hard staying off the booze. Some days it was harder than others, but the thought of having a son kept him going when he felt tempted. He knew from experience that if he just had one that would lead to another and another until he didn't know what he was doing. He couldn't risk that if he had a baby.

'Hey Lovie, Come and have a look at this,' Ellen was like a kid in a candy shop. Behind the bedroom there was a bathroom area. Another sliding door led out from the bathroom to a dip pool next to a huge rocky outcrop. The decoration was rustic in keeping with the environment. On the wide veranda stretching the length of the cabin there were loungers and coffee tables.

'It's just perfect here,' breathed Ellen as she leant her elbows on the balustrade watching a giraffe stretching up its long neck to eat the topmost leaves of an acacia tree.

'Oh look, Dan! The elephants are coming.' A herd of elephants and their young of various sizes lumbered slowly towards the waterhole eager for refreshment. They paused and began to drink, then shambled on to another pool close by which Ellen hadn't noticed and wallowed in the cool water squirting it all over their bodies with their trunks. When they climbed out of the water their bodies were wet and glistening in the sunlight. Then they sucked up sand and blew it all over themselves to protect them from the hot sun, making their bodies turn from grey to reddy brown. 'It's a bit like that time we were at the river and you took us to see the elephants there,' she recalled.

'I remember.' He said softly, 'that's the weekend I fell in love with you, you know.'

Ellen smiled happily 'thank you for bringing us here Dan,' she breathed 'It really is the most heavenly place.'

'You deserve it after all I've put you through,' murmured Daniel into her hair. She leaned her head back onto his chest as he put his arms around her. They both needed this, she thought. A second honeymoon far away from the world to heal the wounds of the past.

'Come on then,' urged Dan. 'Let's spend an hour or two in the park before it gets dark. We might see lion if we're lucky.'

# Chapter 27

AS THEY DROVE along the red sand road they viewed herds of springbok and zebra which skittered away as they passed by. Suddenly the bush was bare and there was nothing but scrub and trees, and a fish eagle circling overhead. They rounded a bend and in front of them were some large boulders by the side of the road. Dan stopped.

'Why are we stopping, Daniel?'

'Just look closely, Ell. What do you see?' asked Dan.

Ellen strained her eyes looking at the boulders and then she saw a flicker of movement as an ear twitched. She looked again. Not just a boulder but an enormous animal lying there next to it. Slowly it raised its great head and she recognized the sharp horn of a rhinoceros. It studied them for a few seconds and then rose from its resting place and wandered out onto the middle of the road, followed moments later by its baby. The mother stood four feet high at the shoulder staring at them with piggy eyes, daring them to come closer. They watched for a while, unable to get past but the animal began to look unsettled pawing the ground with her great hoof.

'She's not happy with us,' murmured Daniel. 'They don't like being disturbed at such close quarters when their babies are around. Time to make a rapid departure I think.'

With that he backed up smartly and turned the jeep around until it was facing in the direction they'd come. The beast sniffed the air and pawed the ground again.

'She's as blind as a bat but unfortunately we're upwind so she can smell us. Hold on tight Ellen, here she comes,' yelled Dan as he put his foot down hard on the accelerator and the jeep shot off down the rutted track. Ellen held her breath as one and a half tons of animal madness came charging along twenty yards behind them. The beast was amazingly quick for its size and was gaining on them rapidly, its great horn threatening to impale their vehicle at any second. Suddenly it stopped dead in its tracks and watched them menacingly as they sped away, dust billowing up behind them.

Ellen let out a huge sigh of relief. That was a bit too close for comfort.

'Sorry Ell,' said Dan apologetically, 'there was no way I could get past her so the only recourse was to turn around. If we hadn't been upwind she probably wouldn't have chased us. Are you alright?' He studied her with concern, afraid that the shock might have damaged his son.

'I'm feeling a bit wobbly, 'she said shakily. 'How about getting back to the Lodge now. I think I could do with some quiet time after that little adventure.'

Daniel grinned, reassured. 'You can always rely on me to provide some excitement in your life.'

Ellen smiled wearily and shook her head.

'You can sometimes have too much of a good thing, Daniel.' she said wryly.

They were within half a mile from the gates of the park when the front nearside wheel began to judder.

'Soddit,' cursed Dan. 'Just our luck. Looks like we have a flat.'

'So *now* what?' This was beginning to remind her of the first time she went out with Daniel.

'I'll have to stop and change the tire,' said Daniel. 'Don't worry. It won't take long.'

He stopped the jeep and hauled the spare wheel and the jack out of the back. He was kneeling down loosening the wheel nuts when Ellen said quietly, 'don't move Dan! We have company.'

Daniel looked up at a female lion crouching in the grass ten yards away. She was very still and stared hypnotically at Daniel.

Dan spoke urgently without taking his eyes off the animal, 'Sweetie there's a rifle behind your seat. Very slowly can you lift it out and hand it to me.'

Ellen did as she was asked and gingerly handed the gun down to Daniel. He took it and backed carefully into the jeep whilst training the gun on the animal, leaving the spare wheel and the jack lying in the road. Just as he was climbing into the cab the lioness crept forward ready to pounce. Daniel hurriedly closed the door.

'We'll just have to wait until someone comes out to find us. She'll probably get fed up and go away eventually if we stay really quiet but it's too risky to get out of the vehicle. We might have to stay here all night. I don't want to use the gun but I shall if it's necessary.' The jeep had a canvas top which could be ripped open by an aggressive lion if it so wished. The chances were she had cubs hidden in the undergrowth and an animal with young was always more dangerous if it felt threatened.

Ellen was worried. She was still feeling a little odd but she wasn't going to mention it to Daniel as she didn't want him fussing, especially when there was nothing he could do.

Making sure her window was closed and her door was locked she prepared herself for a long wait. Night fell quickly as it does in the southern hemisphere, and the lion merged into the background, but Dan kept his rifle cocked ready to fire. They were just beginning to think they'd spend all night in the jeep when headlights came bouncing along the track behind them. A land cruiser halted beside them full of eager tourists out on a night drive. The cheery voice of Hennie shouted across to them.

'Is that you Dan?' A powerful torch lit up the cab dazzling them.

'Yes Hennie. We've got a flat here and there's a she lion wandering around. It's too risky to get out and fix it.'

'Don't worry. Sam here will come and mend it whilst you stand guard.' A young African Game Warden dressed in khaki longs and jacket swung down from the land cruiser and came across whilst Hennie covered him with his rife. He knelt in the sand and jacked up the jeep then changed the wheel and tightened the wheel nuts whilst Daniel swept the light over the bush around them. The lion had now disappeared but it could still be nearby in the bushes. When the job was done Sam got back into the land cruiser and Dan and Ellen followed them back to the Lodge.

# Chapter 28

ON THEIR ARRIVAL back at the cabin Ellen went to the bathroom. She didn't want to worry Daniel but she really was feeling quite strange.

There was a sharp cry and Daniel raced through to see what the matter was. Ellen was straddled on the loo looking down bleakly at a patch of blood in her pants.

She looked up at Daniel and shook her head, 'I think I need to get to a hospital, Dan! I'm bleeding! I think I might be losing our baby.' She began to cry. Daniel was distraught and feeling very guilty. It was all his fault. The shock of being charged by that rhino must have traumatised her not to mention bumping over that rough road, and then the lion incident. It was all too much for her in her condition.

'Hang in there Sweetie. I'm going to phone for help.'

There was no time to lose. Dan frantically raced through to the lounge and grabbed the phone off the wall. He dialled 9 and got straight through to Hennie at reception, 'Hennie I need a stretcher quick! I think my wife may be having a miscarriage.'

'No stretcher but we have a wheelchair, Dan. Sit tight. It'll be there straight away.'

Daniel returned to Ellen and held her hand tightly, 'Hold tight Sweetie, and don't move. Help is coming.' She was looking pale and frightened and he was terrified. He couldn't bear to think of her losing their child.

Fifteen minutes later Dan had gently lifted Ellen into Hennie's old Mercedes and they were on their way to Victoria Falls Hospital five miles away whilst Hennie phoned the hospital to say they were on their way.

When they arrived they were met by a doctor and a nurse and she was rushed through to a treatment room where she was examined straightaway. Daniel paced up and down outside. His face was ashen and he couldn't stop blaming himself. He should have had more sense. Why did he always have to show off how clever he was? It wasn't clever to go so close to a rhino with a calf. He should have carried on. And he should have been more careful on the road then he wouldn't have got that puncture. The list of what he should and shouldn't have done grew longer. He began to make a pact with God

'*Please God keep Ellen and the baby safe and I promise I'll be the best father ever.*' He'd never felt the need to pray before, but this was his child he was praying for and he hoped God would overlook all his frailties and answer his plea.

Ten minutes later a doctor came out and spoke to him. 'Your wife is going to be O.K. Mr du Plessis. It seems she's had a nasty shock which has resulted in a few spots of blood but that's all. The baby is fine. But it's a warning that she needs to rest with no excitement. I advise complete rest for the next few days.'

'Thank God,' whispered Dan. Maybe there was a God after all.

He drove them back to the Lodge and thanked Hennie for helping them.

'Don't thank me,' said his friend. 'I'm just glad Ellen is O.K. Maybe you should relax here for a couple of days and just watch the game from your cabin. There's plenty to see up there and I can arrange for all your meals to be sent up to you.'

Dan nodded. 'Thanks Hennie.'

So for the next few days they just relaxed on the veranda and watched the elephants coming to drink and bathe at the waterholes right outside their window whilst Daniel danced attendance on his wife, determined to do everything he could to make sure his wife and son were safe and well.

# Chapter 29

THE FOLLOWING MONTHS were full of joy and love as Ellen's stomach became progressively rounder. The bigger she became the more Daniel cosseted her and showed her off proudly to his friends. She enjoyed all the attention he lavished on her. It was like it was when they first met. She gave up work at the end of October but was assured by her headmaster that she could return when she was ready.

The only cloud on the horizon was the terrorist incursions on the border which were becoming more and more common each day. Having failed to get rid of Ian Smith, the opposing rebel leaders, Nkomo and Mugabe now billeted their freedom fighters in the bush south of Lusaka where President Kaunda was happy to give them protection from Ian Smith's Selous Scouts who were every bit as vicious as the Freedom Fighters themselves. The terror and the brutality wore on but so far it hadn't reached Salisbury. It was farmers and villagers far out of the town who were at risk. The rebels made frequent incursions from Zambia into Rhodesia to murder white farmers and terrorise innocent villagers whose only crime was to support the opposing rebel leader. It was the ambition of both Nkomo and Mugabe to become leader of Rhodesia once the country had achieved black rule, so it was in each of their interests to recruit as many supporters as possible. They did that through sheer brutality, instilling loyalty through fear. To avoid being abused the villagers took to carrying two party cards; one for Nkomo's party ZAPU, and one for Mugabe's party ZANU They would show which ever card was appropriate when the bully boys came around to knock over their cooking pots and threaten their wives.

Every so often in the city there would be the *chuckchucka* of helicopter blades as a fleet of army helicopters passed overhead telling residents there was yet another brutal battle being fought close to the border. Daily there were reports of farmers being murdered on their farms, their bodies hacked and draped over fences, but in Salisbury far away from the action the residents felt protected and safe with the army barracks on their doorstep. At rugby matches and other large gatherings people were encouraged to report suspicious packages left unattended, whilst schoolteachers, solicitors, businessmen and shopkeepers were all encouraged to join the home guard and regularly patrol their districts looking out for any suspicious packages and incidents, so Daniel spent many of his free evenings patrolling Hatfield.

# Chapter 30

IT WAS CHRISTMAS time and the heat was really getting to Ellen who was due to give birth any time soon. On Christmas Eve she felt the first pangs as she reached up to put a bauble on the tree which Daniel had brought home that day.

'Here, sit down,' said Daniel, helping her to an armchair. 'You shouldn't be doing that.' He was still traumatised by the near miscarriage at the *Sundiata Lodge*

'I'm fine. Don't fuss,' she said holding her back and gently lowering herself into the chair.

'Let me finish it off,' he said, 'and then I'm going to take you out to Meikles Hotel for a smack up meal.'

'Oh no, Dan. Not tonight, Love. Let's just get something out of the freezer. Actually I quite fancy baked beans on toast. I'm in no fit state to go out. I'm feeling tired and I've got nothing to wear that fits for a start.'

And so on Christmas Eve Daniel opened a tin of baked beans and they dined in style on baked beans on toast.

Holly was born on Christmas Day at the hospital, where nine months before Daniel had such a narrow escape. He came rushing into the ward full of boyish enthusiasm, clutching an enormous bunch of red roses, glowing with pride as he looked down at his baby daughter in her cot beside Ellen's bed.

He picked her up gently and felt a huge tenderness for this tiny being, vowing to himself he would always be there for her. He'd wanted a son but it wasn't important any more. Holly would be her daddy's girl and he would keep her safe whatever happened. He would teach her to ride a bike and saddle a horse and there would be ballet lessons and music lessons. At weekends they'd go out into the bush and he'd teach her all about the animals; how to track and how to identify an animal by its spoor. Nothing would be too much for his beautiful daughter. And one day he would walk her down the aisle in a beautiful white gown. His imagination knew no bounds.

'She's gorgeous. Just like you,' he said leaning over and kissing his wife.' Ellen's heart fell like a stone as she smelt the whiff of vodka on his breath. People said you couldn't smell it but she always could. Suddenly this event which should have been the happiest most sparkling day of their lives was tarnished. She was angry. How could he be so irresponsible as to start drinking again at a time like this when he knew what it would lead to? A big black cloud hung over her and she felt alone facing a huge responsibility for her newly born daughter. However, she kept quiet, not wanting to spoil this moment with recriminations for the sake of her child.

# Chapter 31

DURING THE FOLLOWING weeks Daniel continued to be the caring husband and father and she thought that maybe it was just a blip and everything would be alright after all.  He must have just been wetting the baby's head.  He came home when he promised, insisted on helping her bath the baby and even learnt to change nappies.  Ellen had nothing to complain about.

When Holly was a month old Joanne and Dirk came down to Salisbury to sort out final plans for their wedding and to meet the new addition to the family.

'What a gorgeous name for a gorgeous baby,' cooed Joanne as she cuddled her new niece.

'It suits you,' laughed Ellen.  'Who knows, next year Holly might have a cousin.'

'Give us time,' said Dirk.  'Let's get this wedding over first.'  He looked sheepishly at Joanne.  His adoration was apparent.  Ellen was glad.  Joanne needed someone to heal her after the dreadful ordeal of her parent's death.  Maybe now was the time for healing to begin for both her and Daniel.

The day of the wedding dawned with blue skies and wall to wall sunshine. Dirk had stayed the night in the Routledge Hotel whilst Joanne stayed with Ellen and Daniel. The service was to be held at 11am at the Anglican Cathedral in Salisbury and the reception afterwards at the Routledge. Joanne had decided not to have bridesmaids. She'd asked Ellen but with Holly still being so small she felt she needed to be with her. Daniel went off early leaving Ellen and Joanne to titivate and dress.

Donna the hairdresser had arrived and was using heated tongs to roll Joanne's hair into ringlets.

'I'm so nervous,' said the normally confident Joanne. 'I've never been married before.'

Ellen smiled and handed her a brandy. 'Here, that'll sort you out. You're allowed just one. We don't want you rolling down the aisle. Once you're walking down the aisle on Daniel's arm and you see Dirk waiting for you you'll thoroughly enjoy the experience. Your big brother has quite a job on today what with giving you away and then whipping around to the other side to give Dirk the ring. Let's hope he manages not to drop it this time,' she said drily, remembering her own ring rolling around the registry office floor.

'Dirk will donner him if he does,' said Joanne laughing, 'He's driven me mad over the past few months with all these arrangements. You wouldn't think looking at him that he's a closet perfectionist.'

'He just loves you to bits and wants everything to be perfect for you. I must get myself dressed now and sort Holly out quickly.' Ellen disappeared and came back ten minutes later wearing a slub silk turquoise dress and jacket and matching satin pumps, carrying Holly dressed in a pretty little white broderie anglaise dress and bonnet. She looked good enough to eat. Holly was now 6 weeks old and beginning to take note of her surroundings. She happily kicked her chubby little legs and chortled constantly.

'There' said Donna standing back from her creation and putting the mirror up for Joanne to see. 'Is that O.K.?'

'Wonderful. What time is it Ell?'

'It's 10 o'clock. Time to put on your wedding gown.' She went to the bedroom and brought back the dress which had been hanging behind the door in its cellophane cover. Carefully Jo stepped into it drawing it up over her slim frame and Ellen zipped her up.

'O.K. turn around and let's have a look at you'

Joanne looked breath-taking. The empire line gown was simplicity itself and fitted perfectly but Joanne was so beautiful she could have worn a bin bag and still looked gorgeous. The hairdresser pinned a white orchid into her hair and Ellen handed her a simple spray of white roses and orchids.

'There. Dirk will think he's died and gone to heaven. Go knock 'em dead kid.'

A white vintage Rolls Royce pulled up outside. It was time to go.

When the wedding march struck up inside the cathedral Ellen turned around with everyone else to watch the bride walking down the aisle on Daniel's arm. A shiver of pride went through her. They were so beautiful; Joanne, tall, slim and elegant in her simple wedding gown and Daniel, tall dark and handsome in his grey morning suit, silver waistcoat and cravat. She fell in love with him all over again. Even Dirk had scrubbed up well, having shaved and combed his hair for the occasion.

After the service when Dan managed to hand over the ring with no upsets and, much to the amusement of the congregation, Dirk was so bowled over that he stumbled over his words,  they all dispersed into their various cars and drove up the road to the Routledge Hotel. As Joanne and

Dirk arrived in their white vintage Roller there was a cloud of confetti as their friends gathered around them clapping. Dirk proudly helped his new wife out of the car as if she was made of porcelain. He'd loved Joanne for so long and he couldn't believe that she was at last his.

As they entered the foyer the pianist banged out a jazzed up version of the wedding march and the guests all lined up on each side to congratulate the happy pair. After the wedding breakfast Daniel delivered a witty best man's speech amusing his audience with tales of the antics he and Dirk used to get up to, with much good natured barracking from their old friends. Ellen felt a familiar heart flutter as she looked at him, still slim and handsome in his grey suit and matching waistcoat. She hadn't felt so proud of him since her own wedding four years before. Was it really only four years? So much had happened in that time. Not all of it good. But she felt they were now on an upward spiral and everything was going to be alright. Afterwards Daniel relieved Ellen of Holly and went off proudly to show her off to all his old friends whilst Ellen sat and chatted to Joanne and Dirk  before they left for their honeymoon at *Sundiata Lodge* where Dan had taken Ellen the year before.

It was a perfect end to the most perfect wedding day.

# Chapter 32

A WEEK AFTER the wedding when Dirk and Joanne had returned to Lusaka from their short honeymoon at Victoria Falls, Ellen was wandering around the garden cutting roses in the rose garden they'd inherited from the previous owners. She planned to put a bowl on the dining room table to welcome Dan when he arrived home that evening. Holly was asleep in her pram after her midday feed and Ellen was planning to take her to the mother and baby group at the local church hall that afternoon to get to know some of the other young mums round about.

The garden was a mass of colourful blooms in various shades of pink and yellow, red and orange with fragrances a French perfumer would die for. She had already snipped a dozen long stems laden with fresh buds ready to open up, when she spotted her favourite rose hanging limply from the main bush. It needed tying up, so she went to the garden shed in search of some twine. She remembered seeing some in there some weeks before but couldn't remember where.

The shed badly needed tidying out, a job she meant to do during the next school holiday.

She was rooting around behind plant pots and under packing cases when her foot kicked something that clinked. Bending down she lifted up a sack and discovered half a dozen empty half jack vodka bottles hidden beneath it. She was infuriated. How could he drink again knowing how it would affect him? Even if he didn't care about her didn't he consider Holly? Full of resentment she grabbed a bottle and marched into the house completely forgetting about why she had gone there in the first place. Angrily she placed the bottle on the dining room table, vowing to confront Daniel as soon as he came home. She wanted to nip it in the bud. Then noticing the roses still on the kitchen drainer she found a vase and filled it with water then left the flowers on the kitchen worktop. The day was totally spoilt for her. All ideas of attending the mother and toddler group disappeared from her mind. She hadn't the heart for it. Instead she put Holly in her push chair and went for a brisk walk down the road to cool her anger.

That night when they sat down to dinner the empty vodka bottle stared reprovingly from the middle of the table. Ellen had left it there on purpose to see if Dan said anything, but he didn't say a word; just kept eating as if he'd not noticed.

'Aren't you going to ask what that bottle is doing in the middle of the table?' she asked unable to keep the aggravation out of her voice.

'I was wondering about that,' he replied innocently. 'I notice there's a beautiful vase of flowers on the kitchen worktop. Wouldn't that have been more appropriate?' He refused to look her in the eye.

Ellen was frustrated with his denial. 'I found that bottle along with the others under a sack in the shed,' she challenged. Still he didn't admit it.

'I'll have a word with Jonah when he comes in tomorrow morning,' he said. 'They probably belong to him. I'll get him to get rid of them.' Jonah was the gardener they employed to keep the place tidy.

Nothing more was said and they finished their meal in silence. Ellen knew he was lying but she couldn't accuse him outright without proof but she knew it wasn't Jonah. She'd never smelt booze on Jonah before. Resentment was churning inside her. She was sure it had all started again and she didn't think she could cope with it any more.

Things came to a head a week later. She was standing on a chair reaching in the cupboards above the wardrobe for some clothes she'd stored away for Holly as she got bigger, when she came across a full bottle of vodka hidden away at the back. That clinched it. Dan was drinking again. He'd probably started again at Joanne's wedding reception. Looking back she remembered he'd insisted on taking Holly from her and going away to show her off to his friends. She was incensed to think that he'd used their child to deceive her.

That night she waited for him to come home, planning to sit him down and lay down the law. She fed Holly and put her down in her cot. When Dan arrived home he went straight through to the bedroom. She heard cupboards opening and shutting and knew that he was searching for his hidden bottle.

When he came back into the lounge she held up the bottle of vodka triumphantly.

'Is this what you're looking for?' she asked.

Dan glared at her and his face darkened.

'You think you're so fucking clever,' he snarled, his voice dangerously quiet. 'Give it to me.'

He came to take it from her but she stupidly held it behind her. He lunged at her and accidentally knocked her off the chair, in the process hitting her head on the side of the table. Then, without waiting to see if she was alright, he grabbed the bottle and stalked out of the house without a word. She heard his car rev up as he backed out of the driveway at great speed. There was a harsh grinding sound as he scraped the gate and went roaring down the road.

Ellen was shaking. She'd never seen him so angry, and he'd never been physically aggressive before. The charming man she had married was turning into a monster and she didn't know what to do about it.

# Chapter 33

WEEKS WENT BY and Ellen was visiting Liz. She had purposely avoided going there until the bruise on her forehead had finally disappeared and she'd stopped having to hide it with a scarf. They sat next to the pool whilst Liz poured tea and gave a cup to her friend. She had made a milk tart especially for Ellen but the slice lay untouched on her plate. Liz picked Holly up out of her car seat and jogged her on her knee. The child gurgled happily.

'She's a beautiful baby Ellen. You and Daniel are so lucky. Sadly we could never have children,' she said regretfully.

Ellen began to cry.

'Oh sweetheart, what's wrong? I didn't realise you were so unhappy.' Liz put Holly back in her car seat and rushed over to put her arms around Ellen.

'Is it Dan?'

Ellen nodded, taking a tissue from her pocket and blowing her nose loudly.

'He's drinking so much, Liz,' she sobbed. 'You've no idea. He's changed. I hardly know him anymore. I feel as if I'm on an emotional see saw. One minute he's kicked the booze and he's the old Daniel, the one I fell in love with, and the next he's drinking himself into oblivion again and becomes a monster. I thought he'd kicked the habit, especially when I fell pregnant with Holly, and everything was fine for a while, but it's getting worse again and I don't know what to do.' Tears rolled down her cheeks. 'If I dare to question him he becomes nasty and abusive. I really thought he was going to hit me the other night.'

Liz sat down again and leaned forward, grasping Ellen's hands, 'You can't let him hit you and get away with it Ellen. It's the thin end of the wedge and what's more it's dangerous to both you and Holly. If he ever does that again you must grab Holly and come straight round here as soon as you can. Promise me.'

Ellen nodded wearily.

'Johnny and I suspected as much,' Liz continued. 'We've known Dan a long time. Part of the problem with his first two wives was booze but when you came along we thought he'd change. He loved you so much. Believe it or not I know how hard it must be for you, I had the same problem with Johnny years ago.'

Ellen was shocked. 'You?   But you and Johnny are so...together.'

Liz shook her head, 'Maybe now, but there was a time when, like you, I didn't know which way to turn. He drank morning noon and night. I honestly thought he'd damaged his brain. And his behaviour...' she shrugged. 'He was so aggressive. His reputation as a builder went to pot. People just stopped employing him. We had a hard time financially for a few years and if it hadn't been for my job at the veterinary surgery I don't think we'd have survived. He lost job after job, crashed cars, lost his licence and ... well, it was a nightmare. I thought of leaving him many a time. I sometimes think that if we'd had children...' She stopped and sighed deeply, 'well, I might not be here now.'

Ellen looked at Liz in astonishment. She thought she was the only person in the world this was happening to. She couldn't imagine Johnny drunk, but when she thought about it she'd never seen him drink anything other than coke and she'd always imagined there was a brandy in it.

'So what happened to make things right?' She couldn't wait to hear about this magic solution to her problems.

'Well, I found this wonderful family support group. They helped me to see things differently and once I was off his back Johnny eventually decided to join A.A. It wasn't easy and it didn't happen overnight for either of us but it was worth it. Tell you what, let me take you to a meeting and you can decide for yourself.'

Ellen looked at Holly who was gurgling happily in her chair, kicking her chubby little legs.

'But what about Holly?' she said doubtfully, 'I can't possibly leave her with Daniel. I wouldn't be able to trust him to come home on time never mind look after her. He never comes home till after ten most nights and he's always three sheets to the wind.'

'That's not a problem. We'll take her with us,' assured Liz. And so it was settled and Ellen attended her first Al-Anon Family Group meeting.

# Chapter 34

OVER THE NEXT few months she packed Holly into her carrier and attended a meeting each Wednesday night. That was the night Dan had to be on duty at the hotel so she didn't need to tell him where she was going. The first night she went she was nervous because she didn't know what to expect. If Liz hadn't come to pick her up she would have chickened out. She walked into a room to see a circle of easy chairs where a group of men and women of all ages looked up at her and smiled.

An older woman came and took her hand, 'I'm Mary,' she said in a gentle Scottish accent, 'What's your first name?' Ellen told her. 'Welcome, Ellen, and who would this gorgeous young lady be?' She smiled down at Holly in her car seat.

'This is Holly,' said Ellen. 'Is it OK to bring her?'

'Of course,' said Mary, 'the more the merrier. Would you like a cup of tea?'

And although she didn't know it at the time that was the beginning of a positive change in her life.

To begin with she found it a relief just talking to that friendly group of people who really understood what she was going through and didn't judge her. They didn't just sympathise, they empathised and she no longer felt alone. She heard some horrendous stories of abuse far worse than her own, but all these people seemed to have achieved a state of serenity in spite of their problems. There were men and women like herself who's partners had the problem, and parents whose sons or daughters were affected. Some remained with their alcoholic and some had found the courage to leave or send them away but they all had one thing in common; they all wanted a change in their lives.

They told her alcoholism was a disease and that it was pointless her trying to control it. No-one had ever told her that before. Everyone had told her she was responsible, that she should do something about it. She shouldn't buy booze, she should make him go to the doctor, she should take his car keys away, she should leave. So many shoulds. Had any of them ever tried stopping an alcoholic drinking? Nobody told her about the lies and the hidden bottles, the abuse and the fear. Her friends were well meaning but they all made her feel so guilty and resentful. But at Al-Anon she was given support and hope by people who knew what they were talking about.

There was a lot to learn and it couldn't all be absorbed in one meeting but she took on board what she felt might work for her. She stopped sniffing his breath when he came in, stopped asking questions and stopped searching for bottles in the garden shed. If he got caught drink driving she didn't rush to help him or make excuses to his boss, and when he said nasty things to her she tried not to react and turned her mind to something else. There was no point arguing with him when he was drunk. The message was so simple. She just had to let go and look after herself and Holly.

In between meetings she would talk to Liz and Johnny. 'Look Ellen, it might take some time for Dan to come to his senses,' said Johnny. 'It may take a crisis to bring it home to him what he's doing to himself, but in the meantime you can do a lot to help yourself.'

'I know it's hard to let go but stick at it for your own sanity, Ellen,' said Liz. 'Anyone who knew Johnny when he was drinking can't believe he's the same person.' She smiled fondly at her husband. 'I was sure there was no hope for him but without Al-Anon we'd have both ended up in a mental asylum.'

Ellen would always be grateful for those two dear people and the hope and common sense they gave to her.

# Chapter 35

ELLEN WAS A willing learner and as soon as she was told she was wasting her time trying to stop Daniel drinking she started to do things to make her own life more purposeful instead of focussing her whole attention on him and his problem. Tidying out a cupboard one day she came across her old badminton racquet. She hadn't used it for years, not since before she was married. She recalled how Ben had advised her not to give up her badminton which she'd enjoyed so much. When she looked back it became obvious to her exactly when things had begun to go wrong for her and Dan. Right from the word go she'd always been available to do whatever Dan wanted, whether it was going with him on his business trips or helping out with casino nights at the club. Her obsession with him had crept up without her realising it and now she had to find herself again before it was too late. Life wasn't all about Daniel. She determined to do something about it.

The following day she knocked on the headmaster's door carrying her badminton racquet.

'Come in.'

Entering the holy of holies she sat down opposite the elderly headmaster. He looked up from reading a story in a child's exercise book and smiled at her benignly over his half-moon spectacles.

'Good morning, Ellen. What can I do for you? I hope all's well at home.' Mr Mellows was a kindly man who knew all about Daniel's problem. Ellen had arrived at school one day visibly upset and after she'd burst out the whole wretched story to him he'd insisted that she go home and let him take her class for the morning.

'No it's nothing to do with Dan, Mr Mellows. But I've had an idea and I want to run it past you if I may.'

Ellen put her badminton racquet down on his desk. At that moment there was a tap on the door.

'Just let me get that, Ellen. Won't be a minute.' The headmaster got up and opened the door. The muted sound of teachers' voices directing their classes could be heard floating down the corridor. A small girl with a round face and blond bunches was standing there waving a sheet of sugar paper with a picture of her family daubed upon it.

'Hello Sophie. Have you brought something to show me?'

'Mrs Jones said I must show you my picture,' came the shrill baby voice of the year one child. Mr Mellows told her how good it was and thanked her for showing it to him. He came back to his desk and took a packet of gold stars out of a drawer, picked one out and stuck it on the child's work. She beamed with pride.

'There, now off you go back to class, Sophie.'

He came and sat down again.

'She tries so hard that little one. Now where were we?'

'I've been thinking, the school hall is only used for assemblies which is a bit of a wasted resource. How about introducing badminton as an afternoon activity for the older children twice a week. I'm happy to teach it. We could also use it for the staff in the evenings. It would be a good way of bonding. We don't see much of each other outside school hours.'

The elderly Head smoothed his thinning hair with a wrinkled hand and thought for a moment. 'There's no court marked out in there and we'd need equipment.'

'A couple of cheap racquets to start and a box of plastic shuttles, that's all. And we could mark the court out ourselves with some white paint and masking tape. I can get one of the others to help me.'

She'd obviously thought it all out.  After giving it some more thought the Head nodded

'OK then let's give it a whirl.  Just get the paint and bring me the receipt.  We can discuss racquets and shuttles later.' He liked Ellen.  She was a good teacher and he was pleased to see she was using her resourcefulness in a positive way instead of focussing it all on her husband.  He was happy to support her in any way he could.

Ellen went to her classroom feeling as if she'd achieved something for the first time in years.  All it had needed was the willingness to change.

Within a fortnight they were up and running and the hollow slap of a shuttlecock and shouts of laughter could be heard most afternoons in the school hall.  It made such a difference to Ellen's life to be involved in something she enjoyed.  For the first time in years she was doing something for herself and not just to please Dan.  It felt liberating.

The staff agreed to play twice a week for an hour early in the evening plus sessions at the weekends which meant that she could take Holly along too.  Eventually parents asked to join and it became quite a social club.

Six months went by and Ellen couldn't believe how her life was changing.  The badminton club had been a lifesaver on many fronts.  She was happier and more settled now despite Dan's drinking and whilst he sometimes moaned about her spending so much time with other people it was obvious that he had gained a new respect for her. She was getting out and doing something she loved and she began to feel good about herself. An added bonus was that it was helping to get rid of some of the extra pounds she'd gained carrying Holly. As for Holly she was loving all the attention she was getting from Ellen's colleagues and Ellen was loving watching all the little changes in her baby's development. The resentment she'd been building up was gradually disappearing as she began to enjoy life again on her own terms.

The fact that Ellen wasn't looking over his shoulder all the time checking up on him seemed to communicate itself to Daniel and whilst he still drank it ceased to be a major obstacle in their relationship. Ellen was more like the feisty girl he'd married and he liked it. In the meantime he was managing to hold on to his job and do the odd home guard duty, but none of that was Ellen's business any more. She now had a life of her own.

Things were going well for their refreshed relationship until the night when he arrived home after his home guard duty in a worse state than she'd ever seen him, seeming more terrified than drunk.

'What on earth's happened, Dan? You're as white as a ghost.' She panicked as she imagined a terrorist attack on their neighbourhood which was right on the edge of Salisbury with miles of bush land between them and the border.

He was shaking like a leaf. 'I went into another car as I was crossing over the Lomagundi Road on the way home. I'd only had one vodka, honestly Ell.' If he said one it was more likely to be half a dozen but she'd learnt not to comment. She breathed a sigh of relief.

'Was anyone hurt?' Ellen had been waiting for something like this to happen for a long time.

'No I don't think so. It was a young couple in the car....... and a little baby. Couldn't have been more than three months old.'

'My God Dan!' her anxiety increased

He was sobbing now and could hardly get his words out. 'We couldn't find the baby, Ell. She was in the back of the car. It was dark and we couldn't find her.' Tears streamed down his face.

'So what happened?'

'We eventually found her under the seat. I've never been so scared, Ell. I just kept thinking it could have been Holly.'

Ellen was scared, 'Oh Dan. Was the baby alright?'

'Yes, the mother said she was but she's taking her to the hospital to be sure. I just feel so bad. It was all my fault. I didn't see them coming.' He sat down in an armchair with his head in his hands. The doorbell rang. 'That's probably the police,' he mumbled through his fingers.

Ellen opened the door and sighed with relief when she saw Johnny standing there. He must have been sent by the angels.

'Johnny. Thank goodness. Come inside. I think you need to talk to Dan.' Johnny followed her into the lounge and sat down next to his friend.

'What's up pal? Do you want to talk about it?' He looked up at Ellen who nodded and left them alone to talk whilst she went to feed and change Holly before putting her down for the night. An hour later she heard Johnny shouting goodbye and came back to sit by her husband. He seemed much calmer. Johnny had always been able to talk to Dan.

'Ellen,' he said hesitantly.

'Yes, Dan?' he never called her Ellen unless it was something serious.

'I don't know what's happening to me but I want it all to stop. I'm going with Johnny to his A.A. meeting tomorrow night.'

Emily's heart sang. It seemed this accident had brought him to his senses at last. It was just the sort of crisis she'd been praying for but thank God no one had been hurt.

# Chapter 36

DANIEL NOW HAD three years of sobriety thanks to A.A. and Ellen was recovering her sanity with the help of Al-Anon and the badminton club. It was a Saturday afternoon and she was relaxing on the patio in her shorts and bikini top with a James Patterson thriller open on her knee. She watched her four year old daughter splashing around in her paddling pool with her little friend Jessica from next door, whilst Bozo chewed a marrow bone on the lawn. She'd never have been able to relax like this before Al-Anon. She'd always been on tenterhooks wondering what Daniel would be up to next. They had both changed over the past three years; Dan was more responsible and Ellen was far more realistic. She looked at her daughter who was now chasing around the garden shrieking with laughter with Bozo and Jessica tearing after her, and she felt grateful for the miracle that had taken place gradually for both of them.

'Steady now,' she shouted as Bozo jumped up at Jessica and nearly knocked her over, 'Calm down now, Holly. Bozo's getting over excited.'

Holly was a healthy child, full of exuberance, with bouncing brown curls and the warm brown eyes of her father.  One day she was going to be a beautiful young woman.  Ellen would have liked her to have been blessed with the long slim limbs and straight silky locks of her Aunt Joanne, but she smiled fondly as she looked at Holly's sturdy little legs and shiny curls and decided that they were going to be just like hers.  What did it matter anyway?  She was a gorgeous product of herself and Dan.  She smiled as she thought of Joanne.  She and Dirk had been married nearly 4 years now and had a two year old son called Pieter.  They were blissfully happy and apart from Dan, Dirk was the proudest father on the planet.  They came and stayed over long weekends occasionally and Holly loved mothering her little cousin.

Their lives had settled down.  Daniel was attending meetings once a week and he was loving his new role as Entertainments Manager at the Routledge Hotel, whilst Ellen now had a part time job at Marlborough Primary School nearby but she continued to attend the badminton club she'd started at Hatfield one evening a week leaving Dan to babysit Holly.  They'd left their rented accommodation in Hatfield and bought a house down the road from Liz and Johnny as an investment for the future, which they were hoping would be theirs once all this fighting ceased.

Ian Smith made regular broadcasts assuring the country that if they all stood firm they could win the battle, and they all believed him because they wanted to, and things didn't seem so bad in Salisbury anyway. Sanctions had done their damage of course and there wasn't the variety of goods there used to be in the shops, but Rhodesians were resilient people and had rallied to the cause, developing home grown industries such as clothing and shoes with materials that could be accessed locally or from South Africa. The British had called on the UN to blockade the port of Beira in Mozambique which meant that oil tankers carrying oil to Rhodesia were prevented from unloading. But the tankers found other ports to unload along the coast. It was impossible to blockade all of them, so oil continued to get through. Petrol rationing was introduced but it was always easy to get extra coupons, especially if overseas visitors were coming to stay. The policy of encouraging tourism from the outside world was important to advertise the Rhodesian cause, and show the world they refused to be beaten, so life went on, albeit under the shadow of the bush war.

Holly went to a crèche three days a week whilst Ellen was at school but it wouldn't be long before she could attend the infant class at Marlborough Primary where Ellen worked. On occasions they employed Eva, a maternal African lady who worked at the crèche, to come in and babysit when there was a school function Ellen needed to attend. She was busy contemplating her daughter's future when she heard Daniel's car tyres scrunching on the gravelled driveway. He wasn't normally home this early. There must be something going on.

'Daddy, Daddy,' shouted Holly as she jumped out of the paddling pool and ran to meet her father.

'How's my snookums today?' He lifted her up high and she shrieked with delight.

Ellen loved to see them together like this. It made up for all the heartache she'd endured earlier on in their marriage. Things seemed to be going well for them now and she had stopped holding her breath wondering when the next bombshell would fall.

Daniel put Holly down and came and sat beside Ellen.

'This is a nice surprise. Is it our anniversary or something?' she asked laughing.

'No but I have a proposal that I want to talk over with you.' Ellen was intrigued

'Oh yes,' she said coyly, 'What sort of proposal?'

'Well,' said Dan, 'You remember that immigration officer McKenzie we met in Kariba? The one who showed us where the border line was on the Lake?'

'Of course,' replied Ellen. 'How could I forget? Has he come to arrest you at last?'

Daniel grinned, 'Not this time. But he came into the hotel today. I recognised him immediately so we had a chat over a drink. Don't worry Ell, it was only a coke for me,' he said as he saw the shadow pass over her face. 'Evidently he's thrown in his job in Zambia. He said it got boring and he needed a challenge. His kids have grown up and left home, his son is now living down here in Salisbury, but his wife ran off with another man, so he emigrated from Zambia and is planning to buy the Observatory Inn over in Mazoe. The thing is he's asked me to go in with him and manage it.' He looked at her searchingly, not sure of her response.

Ellen didn't say anything for a few seconds. She wasn't quite sure how to respond.

'It's a big change for us Dan. Are you sure you want to throw in your secure job at the Routledge. You're enjoying it so much? And how about my job at Marlborough. We have to think about Holly's future now. Taking risks is not an option?  I think I'd like to think about it, maybe go out and look at the place before I commit to anything.'

'We'll go out there this weekend.  McKenzie's in no rush to get started on the place but I think it's a wonderful opportunity for us, Ell.  Once Rhodesia is on its feet again the tourist industry will be hot and we'll have got in on the ground floor.  At the moment the locals are eager for somewhere close to home and out of town where they can take the family to relax.  It's perfect.'

Dan was hopeful he could get Ellen's backing on this.  He was confident he could make it work but he needed Ellen on board.  However, he knew better than to force her.  He'd put her through enough trauma over the years.  Rather let her chew it over and come to her own decision.  Since joining A.A. he'd done some soul searching and accepted he was a risk taker and a controller, which might have been OK when he was a single man but now he was married with a family he needed to rein in that side of his nature.  He was also learning to share his feelings with Ellen which included how he felt about the accident that had killed his parents.  Now that it was all out in the open he felt less guilty, less shame and the need to drink had left him.  Ellen had listened to him without judging him and he'd come to trust her calm approach to life.  They'd become a team.  It wasn't all about him and he was prepared to accept her suggestions.

He went to get a coke from the fridge and Ellen sat with a frown on her face. Their lives had been so settled for a couple of years now since he'd joined A.A. and she was scared of anything rocking the boat. But she didn't want to puncture Dan's enthusiasm. He was almost back to the Daniel of old but she knew his sobriety hung by a day to day thread. He was only one drink away from going downhill and she didn't know if she could live through that again. Taking on such an uncertain project might just tip the balance.

# Chapter 37

AT HER AL-ANON meeting the following night she shared what had happened and hoped someone would have the answer to her problem. Maybe someone else had had a similar dilemma.

June, a wise old timer, shared her experience, 'I remember something similar happened in my life when Ray had been sober for a while. I thought I still had to be in control, but I didn't. Ray was quite able to make his own decisions. He was a grownup and I needed to let him control his own life. The problem was whether I was prepared to let his decision control mine.'

'So what did you do?' asked Ellen eager to get some feedback.

'Well, I left didn't I. I was so darned sure he was going to cock it all up. I went down to my mother in Joburg with the kids and stayed away for a year. In the end I had to come back. I couldn't manage on my own, and to be honest I was missing him like hell.' She grinned, 'And you know what?

He was still as sober as a judge when I got back, even though everything hadn't been hunky dory for him either. But hey, that worked for me. It might be different for you. But if you stay you need to let go of the fear and trust your Higher Power one hundred per cent. No more dithering for your own sake.'

The following night after she'd put Holly to bed and read her favourite Paddington story she hugged her child tight and turned down her special toadstool lamp so that there was just a soft warm glow lighting up the room. 'Night night sweetheart. Sleep tight and don't let the bugs bite.' She blew a kiss as she left the room.

'Night night mommy. Can you ask daddy to come and say goodnight please.'

'I'll send him right in. Night darling.'

When Daniel came out of Holly's room she patted the seat next to her on the settee, 'Come and sit down, Lovie. I need you to hear my decision.' He sat down next to her and waited on tenterhooks for her to continue. 'I've decided I'll go all the way with you on this project if that's what you decide to do…on one condition.'

'O.K. what's that?'

'I want you to promise that if you *ever* feel you've bitten off more than you can chew, you will talk to me about it.'

He took her face in his hands and kissed her forehead gently.

'Will do. Thank you, Sweetie, for trusting me. I'm going to do everything I can to make you proud of me again.'

Later on, just before she went to sleep, Ellen compared life as it had been in Zambia and life in Rhodesia. One country was so beautiful in its rawness, a country full of adventure and romance. The other a more grown up place where there were problems to surmount and responsibilities to address. She and Dan were about to embark on an adventure just as exciting as their first adventure together on the Zambezi River, and Ellen knew that in order to survive she must let go of her fears and be a hundred percent positive just as she had been on that mighty river years before.

She said a little prayer she'd learnt at Al-Anon; a prayer for acceptance, courage and wisdom and drifted off to sleep, trusting that whatever their future had in store it would turn out alright.

# Chapter 38

THEY STOOD AND stared gloomily at the slimy swimming pool and ramshackled rondavels. The Observatory Inn had been closed for two years and left to rot when the previous owners left the country unable to take their money with them. Africa had crept in out of the bush and taken over again. Grass had grown over the patios of each round chalet whilst the heavy summer rains had beaten holes in the thatched roofs.

Ellen sighed, 'there's an awful lot of work to do before you can even think of marketing this place, Daniel.'

But Dan was more positive. 'McKenzie has money he's prepared to sink into the project. He reckons he can get the place for a song and it won't cost all that much to do the repairs. He knows guys who'll come and do it reasonably cheap. There's plenty of skilled workmen looking for jobs in Salisbury. Once it's up and running he says he's happy for me to buy shares in the place. It's my hotel management experience he's really interested in, not my money.'

'Just as well seeing as we haven't got any,' said Ellen dryly. 'And you're confident you can get it up and running?'

'I know I can. Oh Ellen can't you just see it? Tables and loungers around a sparkling blue pool; all these rondavels tidied up with new thatch and newly slated patios; a restaurant in the main lodge with live music every night; lunches on Saturdays and Sundays.' His brown eyes danced with excitement as he imagined how it could be. 'McKenzie is also thinking of bringing in a few buck and zebra eventually. No big stuff of course just a few animals to give the place that "out in the bush" feeling.'

Ellen had never seen her husband looking so inspired. She smiled, 'And where will we live?' She looked around at the rondavels, not relishing the thought of moving out of her nice spacious house into a small round holiday home.

'We'll stay in our own house of course. It's only twenty miles down the road. I can come out here every day and you can carry on teaching at Marlborough. It's ideal.'

'You've got it all worked out haven't you?' She laughed. 'O.K. you've sold it.'

A month later Dan gave two months' notice to the Routledge and he was ready to start work at the motel.

McKenzie wasted no time getting an army of skilled African workers to go in and clean the place up; builders, plasterers, electricians, painters and thatchers were all bussed out from town each day, and within two months everywhere was transformed.   The rondavels were re-thatched, the patios re-laid with colourful new slate, the pool was cleaned out and given a new coat of sky blue paint with little lights installed in the bottom, whilst the rough plastered walls in the main lodge were given a fresh coat of white emulsion. Finally Ellen was asked to help choose curtains and furniture.   A rustic African theme was adopted for soft furnishings in rich earthy colours.  Large carved animals and tribal drums were purchased from the African market in Victoria Falls to adorn the reception area, with rustic tables and chairs for the dining room crafted by an African carpenter.   At last it was ready and Ellen went to inspect. What a difference.  She could now visualise Daniel's dream.

# Chapter 39

POSTERS WERE PUT up around town, a half page advert was taken out in the Rhodesia Herald and Dan spread the word amongst his customers at the Routledge Hotel, whilst friends and colleagues received special invitations. Very soon they were ready for the Grand Opening.

On the day of the opening customers were slow to arrive. By midday only one or two couples had appeared so Ellen took Holly down to the pool and they sat in the shade of an umbrella with ice-cream dripping off Holly's chin whilst Daniel and McKenzie hung around reception wondering nervously when it would all start happening. Then around 2pm the customers began to flow. Before they knew it people were sat around the swimming pool ordering drinks and sandwiches, and the restaurant staff reported a clamour of phone calls to book for dinner in the evening. Daniel's ship had set sail. He knew there would be storms ahead as well as sunny days but he was ready to deal with them.

Twelve months down the line McKenzie suggested Daniel might like to invest some money into the project. Business was blossoming; people were booking short breaks in the rondavels and the weekend trade continued to grow. He reckoned that with more money they could afford the livestock he was hoping to bring in. So Daniel invested three quarters of their savings with the blessing of Ellen who felt they needed to keep something back in case of emergencies.

To begin with they needed to fence around the perimeter of the 300 hectare property and create a water hole for the animals. This took some months to do but eventually four zebra and four impala were purchased from a game reserve near Kariba, with the option of purchasing more in the future. Daniel, of course, would have liked a couple of giraffe and an elephant or two but that was a little too ambitious. The animals were allowed to roam freely and occasionally ventured into the residential part of the property, much to the delight of visitors who were warned not under any circumstances to feed or stroke them especially the zebra which were known to have unreliable tempers. It gradually became apparent that they would need a trained game warden to oversee that part of the business so McKenzie hired Jan, a retired warden he knew from Kariba, who lodged in one of the rondavels and kept an expert eye on the animals making sure they were healthy and safe. McKenzie also lived on the property, generally keeping an eye on the place and taking care of the business side thus giving Daniel time off when needed, but he was happy to leave the entertainment side to his partner. Everything was ticking along beautifully for everyone.

'Why don't you come down to dinner one night? Bring Liz and Johnny,' said Daniel one day when Ellen complained she never saw him. So she made arrangements for Eva to look after Holly and phoned Liz.

'Get your glad rags on, Liz,' she said, 'We've been invited to a free dinner at the Observatory Inn. Compliments of the Directors.'

# Chapter 40

IT WAS 7PM on a warm September evening when they arrived at the Observatory Inn. Daniel had hired a local four-piece band and a singer to come and entertain the guests on Saturday evenings which accounted for the strains of Petula Clark's hit *Downtown* coming from the main lodge as they drove through the gates and up the driveway between the rows of thatched round chalets. Little lights in the swimming pool sparkled through the water and impala were wandering on the grass verge delicately picking at blades of grass. Ground lights on each side of the driveway lit their way to the thatched Reception building. Inside a pretty smiling African waitress welcomed them into the low lit dining room and led them to a table next to a postage stamp dance floor where couples danced on the spot cheek to cheek. She took their drinks order and left them with the menu. Ellen's breath caught and her heart did a little flutter as it always did when she spotted Daniel's tall slim figure in his dark suit and crisp white shirt. He was still the handsome man she'd married although now she noticed there were a few more creases in his tanned clean cut features.  When he saw them, he smiled and waved, before weaving through the tables to join them, stopping to chat to diners on the way. Ellen was reminded of the first time she saw him at the Kawena Hills in Lusaka years before.  They had shared so much happiness and sorrow over the years since then, but she loved him now more than ever because of it.

'Welcome to my lair,' he said jokingly as he bent down and kissed Ellen on the forehead and shook hands with Johnny.

'Hey, how about me?' protested Liz.  He went around the table and kissed her on the cheek.  'Would I ever forget you, Liz?' Ellen shook her head and smiled at Johnny.   Her husband still had the old charm.

'I must just claim one dance with my beautiful wife and then I must go and charm the other guests, excuse us.' He nodded imperceptibly towards the band and led Ellen onto the dance floor to join another two couples.  Holding one another close they swayed to the strains of *Strangers in the Night*.  Ellen felt safe and protected in her husband's arms. How could she ever have thought of leaving this man?

'I love you Dan,' she murmured.

'And I love you too my beautiful, darling wife, so much.'

He kissed her hair as she nuzzled into his shoulder. They lingered a little longer carried away by the intimacy of their song and finally he brought her back to the table.

'Enjoy yourselves. I'll come back later.' He grinned cheekily. 'Got to go and impress my fans now.' And with that he swept away, in his element, circulating around the room. Ellen smiled fondly. He was quite incorrigible.

They had hardly begun their meal when they heard a disturbance in the reception hall; people were shouting and arguing. Daniel disappeared outside to see what was going on. There was a shot. Everyone in the room stopped what they were doing and looked at one another fearfully. What was going on?

Suddenly a gunman dressed in tattered camouflage rushed into the room waving an AK rifle. He lifted the gun and pointed it at the dance floor.

'Under the table!' screamed Ellen, remembering her terror attack drill at school.

The diners dropped down under the tables seconds before a clatter of gunfire swept the room. After several minutes of silence people began to poke their heads above the tables to see what was going on. It was a massacre. Couples were lying on the dance floor where Ellen and Daniel had been dancing minutes before. They lay on top of one another, some deathly still and others writhing in pain. Ellen's first thought was Daniel. She stood up and began moving towards the door. She had to find him.

'Ellen, get down!' shouted Johnny, but she carried on, her fear for her husband making her lose all sense of caution. Out in the entrance hall someone was lying down surrounded by people. All she could see was a pair of long legs clad in charcoal grey trousers. Daniel! She pushed through the crowd and knelt down beside her husband cradling his head in her lap. He was still alive but blood was seeping onto his white shirt.

'Call an ambulance,' she screamed, panic-stricken.

'It's on its way, Ellen,' said a gentle voice. She looked up and saw McKenzi's stocky form leaning over her anxiously. He looked around at his staff who had gathered in the foyer talking in low concerned voices. 'In the meantime can we clear reception?' he ordered calmly. 'We need to check how many people in the restaurant need medical attention.'

'Where are they?' Ellen whispered, anxiously looking around expecting to see a gunman with his AK pointing at them.

'It was just one guy,' said McKenzie. 'He escaped into the grounds. I think he must have run out of ammunition. I've called the police and they will inform the army to come and secure the area. There will probably be more of them around so we must stay inside and lock all the doors. All we can do now is stay where we are and pray.' He patted Ellen's arm gently. 'Are you O.K. to stay with Dan whilst I look after my staff?' Ellen nodded numbly. 'Shout if you need me. The paramedics will be here shortly.' He got up and shepherded his staff into the dining room. They were all traumatised and were still standing around with big frightened eyes staring down at Dan, too scared to motivate themselves.

The urgent sound of screaming sirens told them that help was on its way and soon four ambulances were lined up outside and paramedics were rushing in with stretchers. They gently lifted Daniel and laid him on a stretcher. He looked deathly pale as the blood continued to drain from him. Ellen followed them outside and climbed in beside Daniel as the doors closed and the siren began its insistent shriek. Inside the ambulance they set up a drip and kept checking his vital signs.

'Don't die my Lovie,' Ellen whispered, holding onto his hand. 'Please don't die. Holly needs you and I need you.' She was weeping as she sat next to him stroking his hair as if by doing so she could prevent the worst from happening.

As they drove hell for leather towards Salisbury with police sirens screaming in front of them they met a number of khaki army trucks coming from the opposite direction, but Ellen didn't notice. She just sat there willing Daniel to live.

# Chapter 41

IT WAS TOUCH and go whether Daniel would survive the bullet that had entered his chest cavity and pierced his right lung. Ellen spent hours outside the operating theatre just waiting for the doctors to give her some news. As she sat on an uncomfortable hard back chair in the bleak corridor she thought back to when she had first met the tall, dark handsome man who had looked down at her with laughing brown eyes by the lily pool at the Kawena Hills Hotel; those same laughing brown eyes that had looked up at her in the tree by the Zambezi River; always those eyes that had at times made her tremble with fear and quiver with delight. The thought that she might never look into those eyes again terrified her. She had experienced both the heights of passion and the depths of despair with Daniel du Plessis. But they had come through it all together and were stronger for it. She couldn't imagine life without this lovable, energetic man. He was her life force and she loved him unconditionally.

'Excuse me Mrs du Plessis.' The gentle voice brought her back to the present and she looked up apprehensively at the green garbed surgeon who was still wearing his green surgical cap. 'My name is Abrahams. I've just completed your husband's operation. May I have a word?'

The surgeon led her into a sterile office where he sat down opposite her and clasped his hands on his desk. Ellen's heart beat painfully, dreading what he was about to say to her.

'What can you tell me?' she asked anxiously.

He took a deep breath, 'Mrs du Plessis, we have had to remove the upper lobe of the right lung which was severely damaged. The good news is that Mr du Plessis has survived the operation but we are not out of the woods yet. At the moment we have inserted a thoracotomy tube; that's a flexible tube inserted between the chest wall and the lung to draw off any blood and body fluids. It also helps to keep the lung inflated. That will remain in overnight and if he survives the night he will be put on antibiotics to avoid the risk of pneumonia.' He looked at her kindly. 'I think you should go home and get some rest now Mrs Du Plessis. He'll sleep now and there's nothing more to be done until tomorrow morning. We'll phone straight away and let you know of any change.'

Ellen nodded and got up. 'Thank you Mr Abrahams, I appreciate all you've done.'

She drove home worrying about Daniel lying all alone in that hospital bed but she knew he was in God's hands now. She went into the empty house which felt dead without her husband's presence. Liz was looking after Holly until Daniel was out of danger, but Ellen couldn't sleep. She tossed and turned until three a.m. when she got up and went and sat in the chair with a mug of hot milk. At seven she awoke from a fitful sleep with a crick in her neck and phoned the hospital dreading what they would tell her.

'Yes, Mrs du Plessis,' said the Sister, 'your husband is awake. He's very sore and very weak but I'm glad to say he's come through the operation.'

Ellen nearly collapsed with exhaustion and relief.

She grabbed her car keys and drove as fast as she dared down to the hospital. As she arrived at Intensive Care she met Mr Abrahams coming out.

'Your husband is awake,' he told her, 'he's looking very sorry for himself and says he wants to go home which is a good sign.'

Ellen smiled. That was so typical of Daniel. She knew in her heart he was going to be OK. He was strong and determined and he would fight in the same way he'd fought every other problem in his life with stubbornness and determination.

'Thank you Mr Abrahams. So when do you think I can take him home?'

'We'll keep him in intensive care for a few more days. If he responds well to treatment he could be out of here by next week. Then, provided that you can assure us that he'll take it easy, we'll release him into your care. But I must stress, no excitement and plenty of rest. He'll also need to see his doctor once a week to make sure there is no infection.'

The surgeon shook her hand.

'Goodbye Mrs Du Plessis… and good luck.'

Ellen pushed open the door to Intensive Care and looked around. There were four beds in there with people hooked up to various machines. Daniel was in the one across the room. She went over and looked down at him. He looked half his normal size and very frail. He sensed her presence and opened his eyes.

'Hi Sweetie. Can't get rid of me so easily,' he said weakly. She took his hand and leaned over and kissed him, tears running down her cheeks in relief.

'Stop messing about and get better soon,' she said brokenly.

He grinned feebly, closed his eyes and went back to sleep.

The following week Daniel was allowed home. He had little energy and needed help to get into the car and into the house. Holly couldn't wait to see her daddy once again but was a little withdrawn when she saw him looking so frail. This wasn't the daddy who lifted her into the air when she ran to meet him.

Once he was in bed she peeped at him shyly from around the door. Daniel called her, 'Come here Snooks. Come and give your old dad a big hug.'

Slowly she crept in and climbed onto the bed whilst Ellen looked on, nervous that her weight might somehow open the wound in his chest.

Daniel put his arms around her, 'I love you my Snookums.'

'Love you too Daddy,' He kissed her on the nose. Then carefully he disentangled himself and Ellen came and lifted her down.

'Come sweetheart. Let's leave daddy to have a little snooze. He's had a heavy day.' She turned to Daniel. 'Rest now, my Lovie. It's so good to have you home. We've missed you.' She blew a kiss and closed the door.

# Chapter 42

NEWS REPORTS FOR the next week were full of the massacre in Mazoe. The army had gone in and scoured the area but the terrorist cell had retreated north into the bush and had likely sought refuge in one of the villages close to the border. The soldiers would comb the villages and if the gun men were still there they would be caught, but that would take time. In the meantime the terrorists were at liberty to attack again.

With terrorist activity coming so close to the city the citizens of Salisbury were nervous. The sale of security systems soared as people rushed to secure their homes, and people who lived on the outskirts were buying weapons, in preparation for an attacked. There was an atmosphere of fear and uncertainty. A lot of people decided to leave and were accused of taking the 'chicken run' by those loyal to the cause, who had deliberately, if foolishly, given up their British passports to take on Rhodesian citizenship in order to show their loyalty to Ian Smith. Now they had nowhere else to go. Rhodesia was an illegitimate regime, recognised only by South Africa.

At the Observatory Inn three people had lost their lives, whilst five were in a critical condition. Daniel had been lucky. Six weeks later with Ellen's care he was much stronger and insisting he should go back to work for an hour or two each day. However Ellen was determined he should take it easy and would take no nonsense from him.

The Observatory Inn had taken a knock on two levels. Not only were they suffering from not having their charismatic manager there full time, they also experienced a drop in custom due to the attack, especially in the evenings when people were loath to travel out of town at night. Families were staying away at the weekends and the pool was deserted apart from a few young diehard couples who hadn't yet experienced the responsibility of children. The staff remained loyal but with takings down it was a struggle to pay them and some had to be laid off. Daniel wondered how long they could carry on. If he'd had the energy he'd have devised ways of attracting the punters back again, but he became easily tired these days and felt half the man he used to be. Ellen was increasingly worried about him, worried about his health and worried that boredom might cause him to pick up another drink, although Johnny assured her that it was unlikely seeing as Daniel had been dry for so long. But you could never say never where an alcoholic was concerned.

Daniel was also worried, not about the drinking but about his family's safety. They lived right on the edge of town with bushland almost reaching their back door and he was in no condition to defend them should the worst happen. Bozo was a good guard dog and would bark at the slightest intrusion but he would be hopeless at defending them. He began to think he should get his family away from Salisbury altogether. South Africa was an option, and England of course. He wondered if he could tolerate the cold in UK. His grandparents had come from England and they'd talked about long cold winters and wet cloudy summers, a far cry from the sunny climate he was used to, but the job situation was precarious in South Africa. However it was more about which option would be best for Ellen and Holly, but he wouldn't mentioned his fears to her just yet as he didn't want to add to her anxieties, for he knew she was concerned about him. The idea remained on hold for now.

In the meantime Bishop Muzorewa, a non-combative African leader, had become President, voted in by a majority of peace loving Africans, and everyone, black and white alike, thought a compromise had been reached and the problem was over. But Mugabe and Nkomo were not appeased. They called Muzorewa a white man's puppet and set their sights on complete control with assaults continuing more viciously than ever.

The attack on a citrus farm the other side of Mazoe six months later made up Dan's mind. The farmer was slaughtered outside his farmhouse, ambushed along with his workers as he arrived home after a day spraying his orange crop. The gunmen then broke into the house and brutally raped his wife. Fortunately for his teenage daughter she was away staying with friends in town. It seemed like the end of the road for most white Rhodesians.

'Ellen I need to talk to you,' Dan said one evening after Holly was in bed and they were watching T.V. after dinner. 'You remember I promised I would talk to you if I had any concerns.'

Ellen rose and put off the television. This sounded ominous.

'Ok I'm listening,' she went to sit down opposite him.

'How do you feel about leaving Rhodesia? Things are becoming unsafe and I think it's time to get you and Holly away from here. Not only that, I'm not sure how long the Inn will survive in this climate of fear.'

'I know,' said Ellen sadly, 'I have to admit I've also been worried, more for Holly than for myself. I suppose I always knew it would come to this sometime and I think now is as good a time as any to leave before the disruption affects Holly's schooling.'

They stayed up late discussing their options. Zambia was out of the question seeing as they were prohibited immigrants, and moving down to South Africa would only prolong the agony. The winds of change were sweeping through Africa and one day it would be the turn of South Africa. In the end Ellen decided to write to her mother and see if she'd have them there until they were on their feet. Her mother was adamant. There was no question. They must go to her. Daniel wanted Ellen and Holly to leave before him but she wouldn't hear of it.

'No, we all leave together or not at all,' she said firmly.

# Chapter 43

### December 1978

THEY DECIDED TO leave Salisbury at the end of the year when Ellen's class went up to their next teacher. Daniel signed his shares in the business over to McKenzie. There seemed no point in hanging on to them as once he had left the country they wouldn't be worth anything to him, and McKenzie could possibly build the place up again with the help of a new partner. McKenzie promised that if that happened he'd find a way of getting some money over to the UK, but in the present climate that was impossible; people were only allowed a small amount out of the country each year. But McKenzie was a good man and Daniel trusted him to do what was best. Daniel's main concern now was to get Ellen and Holly away from danger.

So they spent two months selling up and deciding what to do with Bozo. They talked about taking him with them but he wasn't a young dog anymore and he would have to spend six months in quarantine plus the stress of travelling.

Ellen couldn't put him through that ordeal, so reluctantly she asked Liz if she would keep him. Mischa had died so it seemed the most sensible thing to do and Liz was only too pleased to have one of her babies back again. But it broke Ellen's heart to leave him there. He'd been such a huge part of their lives, one of the family. When she dropped him off with Liz he padded after her to the car and put his paws up on the sill whimpering, as if he sensed she was leaving him. She looked at his woebegone face and was reminded of when he was a pup and his small face had grinned at them through the car window at the custom's post at Kariba. Ellen had to drive away quickly before she broke down completely; she couldn't trust herself not to open the door and take him back home with her. As she looked back through the rear-view mirror she was distraught to see Bozo gazing after her, his liquid spaniel eyes full of reproach, and Liz kneeling down with her arms around him. She couldn't bear the guilt.

There was just one more thing Ellen needed to do before they left. She went to the phone and placed a call to Lusaka.

'Hi Sal. It's me.'

'Ellen, good to hear from you, we miss you. What are you two up to? We've been worried about you.'

'We're good thanks Sal. Dan has recovered well from the gunshot wound, Holly is growing cheekier by the day and I just need to tell you we've decided to go back to England. We're off to U.K. next week. Things are getting bad here.'

'That's wonderful news Ell. We're also set to leave Zambia in six months' time. Ben has decided not to sign another contract. Education here is going downhill so we need to get the kids back home. Darren will be needing to go to university soon.' There was a pause and Ellen could hear Ben's deep voice in the background.

'Ben its Ellen. They're also going back to U.K. like us! Isn't that wonderful?' There was a pause and Ellen heard Ben say, 'send them my love.' Then Sally came back to her, 'I'm over the moon Ell. I can't wait to get together again. We've so much to talk about. We'll let you know as soon as we get there so we can arrange to meet up.' She was bubbling over with excitement. Ellen imagined her friend in one of her home sewn cotton shifts walking up and down with the phone to her ear in one hand and gesticulating wildly with the other.

'Great. See you soon then, Sal. Give my love to Ben and the kids. Got to go. Big hugs.' Ellen put the phone down and her heart felt a little lighter at the thought of seeing her friend again after all these years. Their children would be growing up fast.  Darren, the eldest, would be at least 16.  It had been a long time since she'd sat in Sally's tranquil lounge with her and Ben looking out over their peaceful bushland sharing all her troubles with them.  They'd spoken on the phone over the years of course but it wasn't the same as being face to face.  It would be good to see one another again.

A week later they locked the door of their home for the final time just as an explosion shattered the night air!  The taxi driver switched on his radio and they heard the announcement that the country's fuel depot two miles away had been blown up by the rebels.  The war had finally reached their doorstep.  It was time to leave.

The smoky night sky was aflame as they drove down Salisbury Drive towards the Routledge Hotel where they were to spend their final night in Rhodesia.  As a parting gift Maurice had given them the suite where they had spent their honeymoon ten years before

Once Holly was in bed Ellen went out and stood on their balcony watching the car lights sweeping a path down Jameson Avenue.  Daniel came up behind her and put his arms around her.

'I'm feeling sad to be leaving this place,' said Ellen softly. 'so much has happened here I feel as if this is where I belong.'

'And I've fought my dragons and won with your support,' said Daniel, 'I gave you so much heartache in our early years Ell. Can you ever forgive me?'

She turned to face him, 'Let's rather remember the good times, Dan. I've never stopped loving you in spite of it all. You know that don't you?'

'And I love you too Ell. I know I don't always say it but I do, and I promise that whatever happens I shall always be there for you and Holly.' He pushed the curls back from her forehead and kissed her gently.

'Hey,' she put her finger on his lips, 'no promises, and no expectations. Let's just take it one day at a time.'

Daniel nodded, 'Come. Let's go inside and get some sleep. We've a long day tomorrow.'

# Chapter 44

LATE THE FOLLOWING afternoon a taxi arrived to take them to the airport for their night flight to London. Holly sat between them chattering non-stop, asking hundreds of questions about her grandparents and her new home in England, her little face shining with excitement, reminding Ellen of when she'd first arrived in Zambia so many years before, dreaming of an exciting new adventure in an exotic new country. She envied her child's excitement and optimism.

The heart of Africa now throbbed in her veins. Life anywhere else would seem ordinary in comparison, but she had to approach the change with a positive attitude for the sake of her family. Sadly there was no future for them here anymore. All they had now were memories, but Ellen knew those experiences, both good and bad, had helped to mould her into the rounded person she'd become. She was no longer the innocent girl who'd stepped off the plane into a new life several years before, wearing the rose coloured spectacles of immaturity. She'd grown up and she'd survived.

As they pushed their trolleys through the swing doors of the airport Liz and Johnny rushed to meet them. Liz bent down and hugged Holly.

'Here's something to remind you of your Aunty Liz,' she said. 'You're still not too big to play with soft toys.' She gave Holly something brown and white which looked very much like Bozo and the child buried her face in its fur. Ellen silently promised she would get another puppy for Holly once they were settled in their own home again.

Liz turned to Daniel. 'I'll take care of Bozo and you make sure you take care of this dear child and her mother,' she instructed shaking her finger at him with mock sternness.

'Always,' said Daniel giving her a fond hug.

There was a flurry of farewells and handshakes with tears and promises that they would all see one another again soon. Liz promised to come over and visit but Ellen knew it was probably the last time she would see them for a very long time if ever.

'We're going up to the viewing balcony now,' said Johnny. 'Don't forget to wave.' He dragged his tearful wife away into the lift. 'Don't forget to write,' shouted Liz as the lift door closed, whilst Daniel said a silent thanks to Johnny for making their farewell so short and painless.

They had just booked in their luggage and were about to go through Customs when Daniel felt a tap on his shoulder. He turned round and his face beamed.

'Jo, Dirk. We weren't expecting you.'

'Do you think I'd let my big brother go without giving him a farewell hug,' she said, grabbing him around the neck in a warm embrace with tears brimming in her beautiful eyes.

'Just glad we made it in time. We only decided to come down at the last minute,' said Dirk, holding his three-year old son by the hand. Ellen smiled as she looked at little Pieter. He was a beautiful child with blond hair like his dad, long slim limbs and sparkling brown eyes like Joanne and Daniel. It was a sin for a boy to be so gorgeous.

When all the inevitable hugs and handshakes had been done, Joanne took a flat package out of her handbag.

'I've brought this for you to remind you of the first time we all met. Open it when you get on the plane.' She gave it to Ellen who hugged her again and popped it into her flight bag.

There was a hollow chime on the loudspeaker and they were being called to board their plane.

Dan gathered their hand luggage and Ellen took Holly's hand.

'You folks must come and visit once we're settled,' said Dan

'We shall, and when Dirk gets his transfer to Cape Town you must all come for a holiday,' said Joanne. 'This isn't goodbye. Just au revoir.'

As they walked across the tarmac to their plane they looked back to see Liz, Johnny, Joanne and Dirk waving to them from the viewing balcony. Liz was still blowing her nose into Johnny's big white handkerchief and Johnny was puffing steadfastly on his pipe. Dirk was proudly holding up his son on his shoulders and Joanne was waving fit to bust. It was hard to say goodbye. But they would all carry on their lives and she knew that sometime, somewhere they would meet again. Life had a habit of bringing people together who loved one another.

When they'd buckled themselves into their seats she unwrapped the present Joanne had given her and a piece of paper fell out with Joanne's untidy scrawl on it.

*The love was already plain to see.*
*Missing you heaps J x*

Shona's sketch showed Ellen and Daniel smiling at each other in the first bloom of love next to the Zambezi River with their faces lit by the campfire. Ellen felt tears prickling her eyes. Shona must have given this picture to Joanne on the final day of their camping trip and she'd kept it for years. She remembered clinging onto the branch of that tree looking down at that crocodile. Did she really come so close to death on the Zambezi years before? Once again, she recalled Daniel's laughing brown eyes looking up at her in the tree. She'd been so cross with him for laughing at her but she'd forgiven him as she'd done on numerous other occasions since. So much had happened to all of them since that day; she and Daniel had fallen in love and had a child; they'd lived through his alcoholism and bought the Observatory Inn; they'd experienced a terrorist attack which Daniel had survived, not to mention their many adventures along the way, whilst Joanne had discovered love with an old friend who she'd regarded as a brother. Throughout it all she and Dan had been blessed with such good friends; Sally and Ben, Liz and Johnny, Joanne and Dirk. She wished they could take them all with them.

She turned to gaze out of the window past her reflection into the African night and asked wistfully, 'Do you think we'll ever come back?'

'Maybe, one day, when all this conflict is over.' Daniel put one arm around Holly and the other around Ellen. 'In the meantime we have one another. This is just another adventure and we're going to survive it, I know we will.'

Ellen looked at her husband and smiled. 'Yes, you're right,' she said, 'just another adventure.'

The engines whirred and the lights dimmed signalling they were ready for take-off.

As the plane rose into the night sky Ellen looked down at the lights of the city below which gradually became sparser as they flew out over the African Bush. 'Goodbye Africa,' she whispered, 'I'll never forget you.' Then she opened the inflight magazine and turned to her husband. 'Right, now which cartoon are we going to watch first?'

THE END

# GLOSSARY

**Madala** – old man

**Rondavel** – round thatched hut

**Kia** – servants' quarters

**Boerevor**s – a spicy sausage

**Braaivlei**s – barbecue

**ZANU** – Zimbabwe African National Union

**ZAPU** – Zimbabwe African People's Union

**Kopje** – a small hill

# Acknowledgements

To Matt Nunn, my creative writing teacher who never failed to encourage me, and Kathryn Azarpay, a friend and member of the group, who motivated me to write this novel and helped me to publish it, thank you both  for your help and inspiration.

# About the Author

Jane Maxwell was brought up in the north of England. She studied English literature at the University of Manchester's Teacher Training College in Didsbury and spent the first 12 years of her teaching career in Zambia and Zimbabwe during the fight for independence. Whilst there she travelled extensively throughout the continent and came to love African wild life, experiencing many exciting encounters with various animals along the way. She and her husband returned to England in 1978 where she taught for a further 30 years before retiring in the Midlands. She continues to visit family in South Africa on a regular basis.

www.ingramcontent.com/pod-product-compliance
Lightning Source LLC
Chambersburg PA
CBHW031720170626

46808CB00005B/1819